"Try a little charm.

"Then maybe my daughter will be more reasonable," Ed Welham suggested.

Michael closed his eyes and thought his options through. He apparently didn't have any. Opening his eyes, he smiled grimly. "Have any suggestions?"

Ed shrugged. "Darcy's used to people running away from her. Maybe you could try to get to know her."

Michael swallowed and pushed away his plate. Getting to know Darcy sounded dangerous to him.

Extremely dangerous.

He rolled his sore tongue around his mouth. *Physically hazardous.*

His mind conjured the image of Darcy's dazed gaze as he'd kissed her. *Emotionally lethal.*

A sense of dread sank through him. The battle lines were clearly drawn, but Michael realized his tactics needed revising. "Get to know her. Right."

To survive he'd need a miracle.

Dear Reader,

The first important thing you have to do this month is to flip to the back of this book and fill out the Let's Celebrate sweepstakes entry, then relax and enjoy another good dose of love and laughter!

Popular Jule McBride's debut novel received the *Romantic Times* Reviewer's Choice Award for "best first series romance." Ever since, she has continued to pen heartwarming love stories that have met with strong reviews and made repeated appearances on romance bestseller lists. A recent nominee for a *Romantic Times* award for "career achievement in the category of Love & Laughter" Jule was a natural for Love & Laughter! And I have to admit that when I told her I really wanted a mistaken-identity book, Jule really impressed me with her twist—a pregnant woman who takes over a man's identity!

Trish Jensen is a wonderful new find. Let me quote from the Genie Romance And Women's Fiction Exchange: "Fans of romantic comedy will be delighted to discover new author Trish Jensen, sure to become one of the genre's brightest stars. In her debut novel, Ms. Jensen's sparkling prose mixes love and laughter in an unbeatable combination of wacky situations, off-beat humor and wonderfully memorable characters. I chuckled, I giggled, I laughed out loud...and I hated to see it end. I want more Trish Jensen stories and I want them now!"

Have fun!

Malle Vallik

Malle Vallik
Associate Senior Editor

THE HARDER THEY FALL

Trish Jensen

Harlequin Books

TORONTO • NEW YORK • LONDON
AMSTERDAM • PARIS • SYDNEY • HAMBURG
STOCKHOLM • ATHENS • TOKYO • MILAN
MADRID • WARSAW • BUDAPEST • AUCKLAND

ISBN 0-373-44024-3

THE HARDER THEY FALL

A funny thing happened...

Trish Jensen decided to become a romance writer when she learned the rule about romance writers not having to do housework. Really! It's an honest-to-goodness rule! Well, okay, it was the most creative excuse she could come up with when she tried to explain her theory on dustballs to her husband, Scott. (Dustballs don't kill, people do.)

In truth, she discovered writing on her way to getting an MBA. The MBA has long been abandoned in favor of a computer and characters she argues with out loud. (The dog has finally stopped looking around the room, wondering who she's talking to.) Trish, her husband, dog and cat reside in Amish country, the mountains of central Pennsylvania.

To my husband, Scott, for his unflagging faith.
And for being the role model on which I base
all of my heroes.

And to my parents, Herb and Nancy Graves, for gifting
me with a vivid imagination, a sense of humor and
a romantic soul.

1

DARCY WELHAM KNEW she was in trouble when the grilled tuna landed on the man's lap. High up on the man's lap. Very high up on the man's lap.

"Oh, no!" she moaned. "Not again!"

She tried to grab for it before he noticed. She missed. The mass in her hand most certainly wasn't tuna.

He noticed. He shot to his feet like a missile, knocking her tray out of her hand in the process. Water flew through the air. Before she could yell, "Duck!" he was as wet as one.

Cringing, she chanced a glance at him. His piercing blue eyes narrowed, his ink-black hair dripped water down his face and neck. A muscle in his jaw jerked rhythmically.

Darcy snatched the edge of the white tablecloth and tried to blot at the wet spots on his tailored navy suit. "I'm sorry! I'll...pay to have it cleaned."

The man backed up. Darcy followed, trying desperately to save his designer tie.

The crash of china and silverware stopped her in her tracks. With a grimace, Darcy looked over her shoulder.

The good news was, the candle had been extinguished during its fall to the floor. The bad news was...everything else.

She dropped the incriminating cloth as if it had caught fire. Glancing around the room, she realized she'd captured the attention of every single patron of Welham's Restaurant. Closing her eyes, she whispered a quick, beseeching prayer to God to deliver her from this situation.

Cracking one eye open, she knew her prayer had fallen on deaf ears. Again.

"Darcy…" Tom Murphy, the restaurant manager, said slowly. "May I see you in the office?"

Darcy sighed. Glancing at Tom, she saw the telltale tic begin to twitch under his left eye. That wasn't a good sign. She also noticed the tuna man staring at her as if he'd like to ward her off with a cross. Darcy didn't take offense. She'd grown used to seeing that expression on people's faces. Eventually everyone looked at her like that, including the succession of nannies she'd had during her youth.

"I'm sorry," she said again. "I'll go put in another order for tuna—"

"No!" the man shouted. "I mean," he said, lowering his voice, "I think I'll just have some coffee."

Well, there went another tip, Darcy thought. She didn't think Tom would let her charge the man for his tuna, seeing as it landed…where *did* the tuna go? she wondered, looking around.

Anthony, the busboy, had already started cleaning the mess behind her. He must have picked it up. With another sigh, Darcy retrieved her tray from the floor. "I'll get you that coffee," she said to the man, who was using his handkerchief to dry his face. She moved to step past him, but her shoe landed on something soft and squishy. Her foot slid out from under her.

Darcy windmilled her arms in a vain attempt to keep her balance. The tray in her hand connected with something solid, and she heard a grunt of pain.

Her bottom landed hard on the floor. Thank God her uniform included black pants, because her legs ended up splayed in a very unladylike position. Peeking through lowered lashes, she tried to determine what she'd hit with the tray.

Since the customer was clutching his nose, she thought she had her answer.

Tom Murphy was trying to console the man. Darcy got

a little miffed that he was ignoring her. After all, *she* was the one who'd fallen on her rump!

Well, she did feel bad about the man's nose. If she remembered correctly, he had a very nice nose. In fact, come to think of it, all of his features were quite nice. Combined, they managed to make him very attractive. When he wasn't glaring at her, like he was doing right now.

"I think I found your tuna," Darcy said lamely.

"FIRST, YOU FLOODED the kitchen!"

Darcy sniffed. "That was my first day on the job. No one told me the dishwasher trap had to be cleared after every cycle." She waved vaguely. "I wasn't cut out to wash dishes, anyway."

Tom Murphy stopped pacing back and forth across his office and pointed at Darcy's nose. "Then, you nearly burned the place down."

"You're exaggerating. It was a small fire. And I warned you I couldn't cook."

Tom raked a hand through his carrot-red hair. "The stockroom—"

"That was an accident!"

"Darcy, everything with you is one big accident! Everything!" He threw out his arms. "I thought your father and I were friends."

"Of course you're friends!" Darcy protested. "That's why he sent me here to D.C. Because he knew you'd take care of me."

Tom dropped like deadweight into his chair. "Modeling," he mumbled.

"Excuse me?"

"Modeling. It would be the perfect career for you. You're good-looking. You're tall and slender. You've got great skin...."

Darcy wrinkled her nose. "How dull. Standing perfectly still *all day long?*"

"That's the beauty of it," Tom murmured.

Darcy strolled over to Tom and laid a hand on his arm.

"I'm sorry I've caused trouble, Tom. But you know why I have to do this."

"Yeah, yeah, yeah. Your old man wants you to learn the business from the ground up."

"Right. And, Tom, if I can't prove to him that I can handle the small jobs, he'll never let me run the company. He'll," her voice cracked, "sell to that damn corporation."

Tom shook his head. "Darcy, honey, maybe it would be best if he sells. Do you realize how much money he stands to make? That we all stand to make? I hate to tell you, but most of the employees *want* this deal to go through. If any of the folks here caught wind of who you really are, they'd probably stampede you."

"Why?"

"Darcy, your dad was minutes away from signing the papers before you put a halt to it. All of the employees had already been told about the takeover. They were looking forward to it, with all the added benefits. It's no secret that Ed Welham's daughter was the one to stop the sale."

"You don't think anyone suspects I'm her...I mean, she's me...I mean, *I'm* me, do you?"

Tom grunted. "What they suspect is that I've lost my marbles for not firing you right after the freezer incident."

"How was I supposed to know the chef was doing inventory in there?"

"Let your dad sell, hon."

"It's my birthright, Tom," Darcy said softly. "My mother and father started with one little diner in Spokane and worked their tails off to turn Welham's into the largest chain of five-star restaurants in the country. My mother *died* making this company a success. I can't give it up."

"I know that, hon. I understand how you feel. If it weren't for this dream of yours, your father would have sold out a long time ago. Can't you see that you're just not cut out for the restaurant business?"

"Not the day-to-day operations, maybe. But overall, I can run them as well as anyone. I have an MBA, Tom!" She looked down at the spreadsheets on Tom's desk. Pointing to a row of numbers, she said, "That should be four thousand, three-eighty-six."

Shaking his head, Tom erased the wrong figure and penciled in Darcy's calculation. "Let him sell, Darcy. Then take the profits from your share of the company and do whatever floats your boat."

"I can't, Tom. I'd be betraying my mother's memory."

Tom clucked his tongue. "Okay, honey. But let me just warn you, your father is still talking serious with Dining Incorporated. He seems to think this is just a lark, and you'll get bored or frustrated or thrown in jail for involuntary manslaughter soon enough. In fact, he told me to give this Michael Davidson guy first-class treatment and access."

"Who's Michael Davidson?"

"One of the big shots at D.I. He's going to be hanging around quite a bit for the next couple of weeks."

Darcy hated the man, sight unseen. "When's he arriving?"

Tom studied his nails. "He's here."

"In the restaurant? Now?"

Tom's lips twitched. "That's right, honey."

Her eyes narrowed. "Where?" she growled.

"A few minutes ago he was seated at 6B."

Her mouth dropped open. "No!"

"That's right, hon. You just nearly broke the man's nose."

MICHAEL DAVIDSON resisted the urge to scoot as far away from the ditzy blonde as he could get when she came to pour him more coffee. This woman was a walking time bomb. How she managed to keep this job, he had no idea. The moment the papers were signed on the takeover agreement, his first order of business was going to be handing her her pink slip.

Darcy. Her name tag told him her name was Darcy. Michael mentally added, *the Ditz.*

"Thank God," he mumbled, when she managed to pour the coffee without maiming him.

His nose still hurt, and his crotch still tingled where she'd grabbed him. His hair, for the most part, had dried, but he had the feeling it looked like hell.

He raked a hand through it, combing it with his fingers. Stirring cream into his coffee, he suddenly became aware that she hadn't walked away. He glanced up, arching a brow quizzically.

"How's the coffee?" Darcy the Ditz asked him.

Something jolted through his system as he stared into her glittering, jade-green eyes. He realized that perhaps "dumb blonde" was not an apt description for her. There was intelligence in those eyes. And something else. Something that looked suspiciously like animosity.

"Hot," he said, then almost groaned. He hadn't meant the coffee.

She smiled then, but the smile didn't climb higher than her cheeks. It didn't matter. That smile socked him in the gut. She looked like a young Grace Kelly, with pronounced cheekbones, full, inviting lips, and delicate brows above a pair of the most mesmerizing eyes he'd ever stared into.

He sort of regretted that her hair was pulled back in a tight bun. He'd love to see how long it was. He also cursed the uniform, white blouse under a black vest that managed to disguise her body.

Shaking his head to clear it, Michael looked away. "The coffee's fine," he said, glaring out the window. He felt uneasy guilt, looking into a pair of soulful eyes that would soon be surveying an unemployment line.

It wasn't his problem. As soon as he acquired Welham's, he'd move into the senior vice president's office. This coup would make his career. He'd be too busy to worry about a beautiful, blond tornado.

Besides, Michael already had two too many women in his life to worry about. His heart lurched at the thought. God, he felt like he'd been worrying all of his life. The image of his mother—trying to remain cheerful while working herself into the ground to give her two children the best—lived with him. Haunted him. Drove him. He'd make it up to her. He *had* to make it up to her. He had to prove that those years of backbreaking work had paid off. And this promotion would go a long way toward achieving that goal.

Michael swallowed and turned his attention back to his list.

Still, his waitress lingered. He knew without even looking up. Her perfume scented the air around him, reminding him of flowers and spice all at once. A strange curiosity to know exactly what parts of her body she perfumed popped into his head. Did she spritz the back of her knees? The hollows of her hips? Between her breasts?

The tingling in his groin increased tenfold, and he shifted uncomfortably, determined to ignore her. Sipping his coffee, he went back to making notes.

"It's our own special blend."

"Excuse me?" he snapped.

"The coffee. We blend it here."

Michael made a note. *Have Welham's start buying their coffee from Columbia Bean Company.* Dining Incorporated owned Columbia Bean Company.

"Would you like some dessert?" she asked, her voice sounding strained.

"What?"

"Dessert!" she nearly shrieked. "Dessert! You know, the sweet stuff that comes after the main course?"

Michael looked at her, amazed at her impertinence. He started to reprimand her, but he noticed suddenly that she looked furious. Her cheeks were splotchy, her eyes blazed. And worse, the hand holding the coffeepot was shaking.

He pointed at it. "Put that thing down!"

"What?"

"The coffeepot! Put it down!" he barked like a drill sergeant.

She did. Almost completely on the table. But not quite

enough. As if in slow motion, he watched it begin to teeter precariously toward her.

He didn't know how he got out of his chair. He didn't know anything except that one second he was watching the beginning of another catastrophe, the next he'd pushed her away from the table and shielded her with his body from the scalding liquid.

He knew it was scalding, because he felt it splash against the back of his slacks. Scalding, all right. Scalding his calves.

He closed his eyes and mouthed a foul word.

He slowly became aware that he was still holding her. The burning of his calves faded in his consciousness as he felt another kind of burn where her breasts were pressed to his chest. Even through the layers of clothing between them, he could feel their fullness, their tautness.

She really was slender. He almost felt he could wrap his arms around her twice. Her forehead was level with his aching nose, which meant she had to be close to five-ten or so. Tall. Tall and thin with really, really great breasts.

And her scent wrapped around him, fogging his usually orderly, precise mind. A rush of colors exploded in his head. The golden silk of her hair. The cream velvet of her complexion. The rosy blush of her lips. The moss green of her eyes. Her snapping eyes. Her angry eyes.

"You can let go of me now," she demanded.

Michael released her abruptly. "You're welcome."

Her mouth popped open a little. "I'm welcome?" she growled...just like an angry kitten. "*I'm* welcome?"

"Lady, I just saved you from a few third-degree burns. The least you could do is appreciate it."

"It wouldn't have spilled if you hadn't ordered me...*ordered me* to put it down!"

She had a nasty habit of repeating herself. "Listen, Calamity Jane—"

"The name's Darcy." She leaned sideways and looked behind him. "Thank you, Anthony," she said, with a genuine smile of gratitude. One, he felt, that should have been bestowed on him a few moments ago.

"Darcy, what?" he grilled. He was going to talk to Tom Murphy, *now*.

"Wel—Wellington," she barked back.

"Well, Darcy Wel-Wellington. You are a one-woman disaster zone."

Her chin came up, but it trembled a little. That slight tremble was his undoing. His little sister's chin did exactly that, right before she started to cry. If there was one thing he couldn't stand, it was a crying woman. "Don't you dare start bawling on me!" he ordered.

Her eyes misted.

Damn!

"I won't! I don't cry!"

He liked that in a woman. He released his breath, realizing he'd been holding it in anticipation of crocodile tears. "Listen, I'm sorry." He massaged the back of his neck. "The coffee probably was my fault."

She stared at him in surprise. Then she smiled a little. "Would you like some dessert? All of it is homemade, right here. We have apple-tomato pie and pecan-rhubarb pie and coconut cheesecake and strawberry tortes and brownie surprise and—"

"Pecan pie," he interrupted, half-afraid the pie would land on his head, but also feeling a strange need to make her happy. "Please."

Her smile did look happy then. He liked it. A lot.

"One pecan pie, coming up. More coffee?"

"No!"

She nodded, apparently accustomed to people screaming desperately at her. As she walked away, he admired the sway of her hips. Shaking his head, he turned back to the table. The busboy—Anthony he thought she'd called him—was just rising from where he'd been scrubbing the coal-gray carpet.

Michael pulled his wallet from his breast pocket and took

out a twenty. Slapping it into Anthony's hand, he said, "You deserve this."

Anthony grinned. "To tell you the truth, Darcy's the best thing that ever happened to me. People slip me sympathy tips all the time."

"Combat pay," Michael murmured.

Anthony began to turn away, but abruptly turned back. "But she's one of the sweetest people I know."

Michael admired Anthony's loyalty, and slapped him on the arm. Then he sat down and returned to his notes. *Have Welham's start buying their desserts from Sweet Nothings,* he wrote.

He hesitated. *Fire Darcy Wellington,* he added underneath it.

"WHY HAVEN'T you fired her?"

Tom Murphy's eyes darted around the room, as if he sought escape. "Why would I fire her? She's reliable, she's enthusiastic, she's…"

"Lethal," Michael supplied dryly.

Tom dropped into his chair. It groaned under his weight. "She's a little clumsy, yes. But is that a reason to fire her?"

Michael laughed. "Do you know what she did today? She blew up the espresso machine."

Wincing, Tom said, "I heard."

"She averages one broken plate and two broken glasses per hour. What's it costing you to replace all of that tableware?"

"We're getting volume discounts, though!" Tom said brightly.

Michael's eyes narrowed. Something was wrong with this picture. He'd been in D.C. a week. Long enough for even the biggest idiot to realize Darcy Wellington presented a health risk to employees and customers alike.

True, she was gorgeous. She was even disarmingly charming—to everyone but Michael. She didn't spare an ounce of charm for him. He had the feeling she knew she'd get canned the moment the ink was dry on the takeover papers.

What really had Michael baffled, though, was Darcy's popularity. The employees really liked her...from a distance. And her rueful smile usually made even the angriest customer forgive her. And for some reason he couldn't fathom, Tom Murphy—touted as one of Welham's best general managers—willingly let profits nosedive for the sake of Darcy's employment.

One explanation cut through Michael's mind. "Are you sleeping with her, Murphy?"

Jumping to his feet—gracefully for a man of his size— Tom nearly bellowed, "How dare you suggest such filth, you—"

"I'm sorry," Michael said quickly. "That was out of line. I'm just trying to understand this."

Tom Murphy's outrage had been swift and strong enough to give Michael his answer. And for some reason, Michael felt relieved.

"She's a kid!" Tom continued, obviously not mollified.

"She's twenty-five years old. She's a woman." Michael felt his body go taut, just saying those words. Every sensory detail of Darcy in his arms was etched indelibly in his mind. She was a woman, all right.

Michael cursed himself silently for allowing his thoughts to turn sexual. Sex and business didn't mix. Ever. He'd gotten as far as he had in his thirty-one years by remembering that at all costs.

He grabbed back control of his libido and put a lock on it. Moving to the door, he said, "Tom, I don't know if you've just gone soft, but I promise you this. The moment D.I. takes over, Darcy Wellington is history."

DARCY WAS FURIOUS. Absolutely furious. She stormed to Tom's office and flung open the door without knocking. It hit the wall with a satisfying thud. She thought she heard another muffled sound, but she was too angry to pay it any mind.

Glaring at Tom, she plunked her hands on her hips. "I'm going to shoot that no-good snake right between his baby blues!"

"Darcy—"

"Do you know what he's doing?" she shrieked. "Do you? He's *watching* me. Every move I make—"

"Darcy—"

"And as soon as I make one little mistake, he pulls out his damned notepad and *writes it down!*"

"Darcy—"

"I have half a mind to call my father and have him sell the damned restaurants on the condition that they fire Michael Davidson. Do you know what it's like trying to pour a bowl of soup when that jerk is *staring* at you, just waiting to catch you doing something wrong?"

"Darcy—"

"I hate him! I don't care that everyone thinks he's a hunk. I hate him and I hate having him here! Can't you make him go away?"

"Darcy—"

"If he keeps it up—" Tom's florid face finally registered. "What?"

Tom pointed over her right shoulder. Darcy turned, pretty certain of what she'd find.

At first, all she saw was the open door. Then it slowly swung shut, revealing Michael Davidson. A welt had started forming high on the right side of his forehead, and Darcy had the sinking feeling she knew how he'd gotten it.

"Uh-oh," she muttered.

"Ms. Welham, I presume," Davidson drawled.

O-o-oh, she hated his smug good looks. She hated his power suits. She hated his sensual lips. And most of all she hated his body. His tall, lean body that had started haunting her dreams, ever since the day he'd held her in his arms.

Her chin jerked. So, she was busted. Maybe it was just as well. At least the toad would know who was really in charge around here. Well, sort of in charge. Well, indirectly in charge. "That's right, Mr. Davidson. Darcy Lynn Welham. Future owner of this restaurant."

She flung her arm wide to encompass her domain. Too late, she realized her hand was heading directly for his head. Good thing he had fast reflexes. He ducked just in time.

Darcy snatched her hand back, horrified she'd almost smacked him.

Michael Davidson straightened, glaring at her.

Going on the offensive, she glared right back. "So, you might as well pack up and slither back to whatever hole you call home, Mr. Davidson. Because you're not getting your hands on my restaurants!"

He stepped forward until they were nearly nose-to-nose. "That's where you're wrong, Darcy. D.I. *is* buying the Welham's restaurant chain."

"Over my dead body!"

"You keep blowing up coffeemakers, and that shouldn't take long."

"That machine was faulty!"

"Right," he said, smirking.

Oh, she itched to wipe that smile off his face. Preferably with her palm. *You're a nonviolent person, Darcy,* she reminded herself. She switched tactics. Smiling, she batted her eyelashes. "Can't we be friends?" she asked sweetly.

He looked stunned for a moment. His eyes went wide, and his Adam's apple slipped up and down his throat a couple of times.

Unfortunately, he recovered rather quickly. His smile was lethal. "Not on your life, sweetheart. You've just been upgraded from a walking menace to the enemy. And don't you forget it."

Darcy resisted the urge to kick him in the shin. She raised her nose in the air and sniffed loudly. "My shift's over, Tom. I'm going home."

As she started to march past the creep, she stepped on his foot.

"Ouch!" he yelped. "You did that on purpose!"

She hadn't, but she decided not to admit it. She smiled, then kept right on walking.

"Darcy…" Davidson said, with an ominous ring to his voice.

"What?" she snapped without turning around.

"Remember this. This is war. You are the enemy. And I take no prisoners."

Darcy did turn then, but she focused her attention on Tom. Smiling sweetly, she said, "Tom, did I tell you I spilled Mr. Davidson's entrée on his lap last week?" She waved, her eyes beaming innocence. "It was an accident, of course. I tried to grab it, but I missed." She nodded encouragement. "Ask me how I know I missed."

"I don't think—"

"Come on, Tom. Ask me."

"How did you know you missed?" Tom asked in a reluctant croak.

"Because," she said with a flourish, "he ordered tuna, not shrimp."

Ignoring Davidson's choked sputters, she whirled and left the office.

War, indeed.

2

THREE DAYS LATER, Darcy walked into the break room that doubled as the stockroom. Michael Davidson was hanging a colorful chart on the wall. The title across the top read: Sales Per Customer. Listed down the left side were the names of all of the waiters and waitresses. Horizontally he'd listed the dates for each week they'd worked.

"What do you think you're doing?" Darcy asked.

"Motivating the wait staff," he answered, without looking at her.

"They're not your staff to motivate."

"They will be soon enough." He turned, pinning her with his deep blue gaze. "And the sooner you get used to the idea, the better off they'll all be."

He bent and picked up another large sign, dismissing her.

Darcy fumed. The man was *such* a jerk. And there wasn't a thing she could do about him, according to Tom. Not yet, at any rate. But soon, he'd get his.

She looked at the poster he was busy hanging. This wasn't a chart, but a quote.

I Don't Know What Your Destiny Will Be, But One Thing I Know: The Only Ones Among You Who Will Be Really Happy Are Those Who Will Have Sought And Found How To Serve.

—Dr. Albert Schweitzer.

"You've got to be kidding me! You think hanging up posters of stupid platitudes is going to motivate people?"

He didn't answer her until he'd finished. "The ones who understand them. Do you want an interpretation?"

"You—you—"

He sliced a hand through the air, cutting her off. "Listen, Princess. You might be quite proud of yourself for crooking your finger and bringing a buyout to a grinding halt, but I assure you, it's temporary. The sooner you realize this takeover is best for *everyone*—including you, I might add—the better."

Her retort, when she finally thought of one, was cut off by the entrance of Wendy Walker, another waitress.

"Oh, there you are!" Wendy chirped, sashaying over to Davidson. She tiptoed crimson nails up the sleeve of his banker gray suit coat. "You never answered my question, earlier. Do you want to come to Clyde's with us tonight, or not?"

Darcy resisted the urge to throw up. Wendy was a very nice woman, when with other women. It was only when a man appeared that she turned into a cooing vamp. And men fell at her feet. Or more appropriately, drooled over her…endowments.

For some reason, Wendy's flirtation with the creep bothered Darcy more than it had ever bothered her with any of the other men at Welham's. Maybe because she hated validation that he was an extremely attractive man…when he kept his mouth shut.

Darcy jerked a glass of soda to her lips and glared at the oaf, waiting for him to return Wendy's banter. When his eyes turned ice-blue, and he smoothly moved out of touching distance, she felt oddly relieved.

"Thanks, but no," he replied coolly.

Wendy pouted. "Are you sure?"

"Very."

With that, he left the room.

Wendy watched him go, then turned to Darcy. "He's gay."

Darcy almost choked on her soda. "Michael Davidson?"

Nodding, Wendy said, "Has to be. Five of us have tried to get him out on the town, and he hasn't accepted once. The man has to be gay."

Gay? Darcy didn't believe for a moment that Michael

Davidson was gay. Fastidious, yes. A real, royal pain, yes. But definitely not gay.

She didn't know how she knew this with such certainty. She had very little experience with men, and almost none with their desires. But something about the way he looked at her told Darcy that he was well aware she was a woman. And that he appreciated that fact thoroughly.

Of course, that could just be her imagination. Maybe she read a flare in his eyes that wasn't really there. The rest of his face certainly didn't approve of her. His lips were continuously pursed in a frown, his eyebrows inevitably raised up in mockery.

And the man *did* walk around the restaurant almost like a robot, ignoring all attempts at teasing by the bolder female employees. But on the occasions when Davidson trained all of his disgusting, unnerving attention on her, something burned in his cobalt eyes. Something that made her nerves flutter.

Davidson was definitely heterosexual.

But who was she to voice her opinion on the matter? she thought, as she looked at the chart and motivational poster. So, Michael Davidson had decided that spouting platitudes would be inspirational? What a wonderful idea. Darcy spun and left the room, in search of poster board and a pen.

MICHAEL GLARED at the poster on the wall beside his chart.

Q: What Is Six Inches Long, Two Inches Wide, And Makes Men Act Like Fools?
A: MONEY.

—Anonymous

Tacking up his next chart, Table Turnover Ratios, Michael swore under his breath. He had no doubt who'd put up that poster. He tore it down.

The next day another one had taken its place.

The More I See Of Men, The More I Like Dogs.
                                        —Germaine de Stael

He stalked out of the break room. This was war, all right. All-out war.

DARCY CROSSED her arms belligerently while she watched Davidson tack up yet another chart. This one was titled Breakage Chart. And beside it, where her quote about men and dogs had once hung, was yet another stupid platitude.

Happiness Is A By-Product Of An Effort To Make Someone Else Happy.

                                        —Greta Palmer

Darcy snorted. "If you want to make this someone happy, you'll disappear, Davidson."

He glanced over his shoulder. "Likewise, Wel—" He stopped, looking past her. "Wellington."

Darcy turned and found Wendy behind her. Wendy's big blue eyes went wide, probably in shock over Darcy's impertinence. Darcy didn't care. She was too angry to care. She turned back to him, scowling. "What are you going to do, put gold stars by the winners?"

The next day there were gold stars by the winners' names. He'd pasted three beside Darcy's name on the Breakage Chart.

Davidson smiled at her as he departed from the break room.

Wendy sighed. "What a waste of hunky man."

Darcy wanted to scream. Instead she turned to Wendy with an innocent smile. "Oh, I don't know about that. Davidson's not all that great."

"Are you blind, woman?"

"Did you know he adds extra padding to the shoulders of his suits?"

"No!"

Darcy nodded. "And don't tell anyone, but I've heard he wears lifts in his shoes."

MICHAEL GLANCED down at his checklist. "If we start buying our wine in quantity from our select vintners for *all* of the restaurants, instead of allowing each restaurant to order for itself, we'll save a bundle."

Tom Murphy nodded. "I suggested that to Ed many times. He didn't want to be bothered."

Checking off the item, Michael moved his pencil down the list. "Ditto with the desserts. We can save plenty by contracting with Sweet Nothings."

Tom frowned. "You mean, give up the desserts currently on the menu?"

"Right. Sweet Nothings makes damn good desserts."

"Our desserts are what got us where we are, Davidson. That's what Welham's first became famous for. I think changing that would be a big mistake."

"You're right," Michael said, after some consideration. He crossed that item off his list. "Ed made his name creating some of those offbeat recipes."

"Ed didn't create them."

Michael looked up. "Oh. His wife, then."

"Nope, not Jeannie, either." Tom smiled slightly. "Darcy created them."

"Darcy?" Michael repeated dumbly.

Tom's grin grew wider. "That's right. I think she was ten when she created the coconut cheesecake."

"You're kidding. That's Welham's biggest seller."

"That's right. She can't cook worth a damn, mind you. But she knows how to throw flavors together. It's almost uncanny. Most of the desserts, and a few of the entrées, Darcy created."

Michael tried to adjust to the news, and failed. Until that moment, he'd have guessed that Darcy Welham was a useless ornament in the scheme of things. A beautiful ornament, to be sure. But useless nonetheless.

If Darcy realized what a positive effect she'd had on the

success of Welham's, no wonder she wanted to hang on to the restaurants so badly. Well, that wasn't his problem. His problem was getting Ed Welham to part with them.

He looked down at his list, dismissing the twinge of guilt that pricked him. "About the uniforms..."

"What about them?"

"I like them, don't get me wrong. On the men they've got just the right touch of class. But on the women, I don't know."

"What would you change?"

Michael looked up. "Something more...feminine, I think. Not sexy, but feminine."

Lips twitching, Tom said, "I'm surprised you've noticed."

Michael frowned. "How could I help but notice?"

"Well, I've overheard a few complaints from some of the female employees. Apparently, they don't think you notice enough."

Chuckling, Michael sat back. "Are you referring to the rumor that I'm gay?"

A startled hiss rushed from Tom's lips. "You know about that?"

"Of course."

Tom's eyes narrowed. "You don't look too upset."

"Upset?" Michael laughed. "Are you kidding? I'd encourage it if I knew how."

"Why?"

Sighing, Michael said, "It saves me a lot of hassle. I don't believe in mixing business and pleasure. Unfortunately, some women don't give a damn what I believe. So, this is just...easier."

"I hate to tell you, but Darcy doesn't believe it for a second," Tom told him. "In fact, I think her exact words were, 'If that man is gay, I'm Julia Roberts.'"

Something rocked his system every time Michael heard Darcy's name. Something that irritated him thoroughly. That *something* was physical desire. Beyond all reason, he was attracted to the woman who was trying to ruin his career.

The females grumbling about his lack of interest were right on the money. He had no interest whatsoever in any of them. His feelings concerning the women's uniforms stemmed solely from his desire to see Darcy Welham in something other than slacks, vest and tie. He realized it was a totally unbusinesslike craving, and that, in itself, was enough to make him furious with her.

He stretched out his legs and crossed his ankles. "To tell you the truth, I was wondering if she wasn't the one to start the rumor."

Tom grunted. "That just goes to show how little you know about Darcy. She'd never start a rumor like that."

Michael grunted right back at him. "She started the rumor that I wear elevator shoes," he retorted, still feeling the insult.

Tom waved. "That was just a little joke."

Pointing at the man, Michael said, "I overheard her talking to one of the waitresses in the break room. I heard Darcy tell the girl I have big ears."

Tom did a poor job of stifling a snort of laughter.

"And that my nose is too long," Michael added, his indignation growing. "And that I pad the shoulders of my suits!"

By this time Tom's laughter had turned to guffaws. He slapped his knee. "Well, it's the least you deserve after posting that Breakage Chart."

Michael opened his mouth, but the crashing of the office door against the wall interrupted him. He winced, praising God that he wasn't standing behind it this time.

Darcy stood on the threshold, her eyes blazing green fire. Her chest heaved with indignation and the hand she pointed at him shook. But what really caught Michael's attention was her hair. For the first time, he saw it out of a bun. In thick, glossy waves, it fell nearly to her waist.

"I have a bone to pick with you, Davidson," she said, her voice low and shaky.

Michael regulated his breathing and slapped a bland expression on his face. "It wouldn't be the same bone your customer nearly choked on yesterday, would it?"

He knew it was an unfair attack on her, because Darcy certainly hadn't stuffed the bone down the man's throat. In fact, she'd surprised Michael by quickly and easily performing the Heimlich maneuver on the customer, effectively saving his life. Still, Michael felt a strange need to distance himself from her, to keep the wall of antipathy firmly in place. If he didn't, his only other option would be to stand up and walk over to her, tangle his hands in that thick fall of hair and kiss those full, sassy lips.

He settled for the standing part, tossing his legal pad on Tom's desk.

"You slimy, no-good reptile," Darcy breathed, taking a jerky step into the office. "How could you?"

"Now, Darcy," Tom said, scrambling to his feet. "Just relax."

Michael understood the concern in Tom's voice. When agitated, Darcy Welham was a tall, blond, nuclear bomb.

Darcy ignored him, her eyes trained murderously on Michael. "If I had a gun, I'd shoot your condescending hide from here to Baltimore," she threatened.

Only if you were aiming for Tom, Michael thought, but decided not to say. Something in the gleam of her wild eyes told him she was seriously upset. He had no idea what he could have done to cause it. But if whatever had upset her was indeed his fault, he knew he'd do anything to take it back, make it right.

Females in distress were his downfall. Even females he didn't like. It was his one major weakness, one he'd developed at the ripe old age of eight, when his old man had deserted the family, leaving Michael to care for his mother and sister.

"Tom, would you excuse us for a minute?" he said quietly. "I think Darcy and I need to talk privately."

Tom almost tripped over his feet in his eagerness to comply. Michael waited until he heard the click of the door before asking, "Okay, Darcy, what's this all about?"

She stalked toward him. Michael resisted an overwhelming urge to shield himself behind Tom's desk.

Stopping mere centimeters away from trampling his Ferragamos, she plopped her hands on her hips. "As if you didn't know, you...you—"

"I've got no idea what you're talking about, Darcy," he said quickly, before she could formulate a list of new names. "Tell me what's happened."

Unfortunately, her eyes filled with moisture. "Everyone knows," she choked out.

"Don't cry!"

Obediently, she blinked back her tears.

Breathing relief, he asked, "Everyone knows what?"

"Who I am," she whispered miserably. "You told them who I am, and now everyone hates me."

His heart reached out to hers. He took her shoulders. "It wasn't me, Darcy."

She either didn't hear him, or decided to ignore him. "For the first time in my life I felt accepted somewhere, like I honestly had friends. And you *ruined* it."

He squeezed her shoulders. "It wasn't me. I haven't discussed your connection to Welham's with anyone here except Tom."

For some dumb reason, he felt desperate to make her believe him. How could she even *think* he'd do something that blatantly cruel? True, he had every intention of taking the restaurants from her, but that was strictly business. And she'd benefit, anyway. She'd be one rich young lady when the deal went through.

"Who else could it have been? No one but Tom knows. And I *know* Tom would never tell anyone."

He shook his head. "I don't know, Darcy, but it wasn't me. I swear it."

Her lush lips trembled. "It doesn't matter. They h-hate me now."

The heartache in her eyes nearly sliced him in two. "I'm sorry," he whispered.

Without thinking about it, he slid his hands over her collar, lost in the glistening green of her eyes. "I'm sorry," he repeated softly.

"What am I going to do?"

He didn't know if she was actually asking him, or just wondering out loud. And he didn't have a clue how to answer her because, at the moment, he was struggling with what *he* was going to do. He was going to kiss those trembling lips.

Michael cursed softly before settling his mouth over hers. He glimpsed her startled expression, heard the soft intake of breath, but that didn't stop him. He was way beyond clear thought at the moment. All he wanted, all he cared about was her lips, soft and parted beneath his.

His gut clenched tightly at his first taste of her. She tasted like a sexy combination of mint and woman. He cupped her neck, his thumbs skimming over her jaw. Tilting her head he slanted his lips over hers and coaxed them farther apart.

Her hands clutched his suit, and Michael braced himself for her to shove him away. She didn't. Instead, a little sigh sounded in her throat and her lips grew more relaxed and malleable beneath his.

His body responded to the sound and feel of her surrender with a power that surprised him. He went hot and hard all over.

Pressing deeper, he brushed his mouth over hers more insistently, more frantically. He was losing control. Worse, he didn't care.

"Darcy," he whispered. He lifted his head slightly and watched her eyes flutter open. A wealth of emotions gleamed in their depths: passion, fear, pleasure and confusion.

The beauty of her swollen lips twisted his heart in knots and tore his good sense to shreds. He covered her mouth with his again while he wrapped her hair around his hands.

His senses flamed, his mind reeled. Tipping her head to the side, he pressed her lips farther apart and plunged into her mouth.

Her body snapped stiff.

Pain exploded in his mouth as her teeth bit into his tongue.

Michael reared back, swearing. "Ouch! You bit me!" He shook his hands to free them of her tangling hair.

"You stuck your tongue in my mouth!"

He examined said tongue with his fingers. It felt as swollen as the Goodyear Blimp. "That'th called a Fwench kith, you twit!"

"I know what it is," she said, sticking her nose in the air. "I just wasn't expecting it."

"A thimple 'no, thank you,' would have worked jutht fine."

"No, thank you," she retorted, her eyes flashing.

"Now she tellth me."

Her fists hit her hips again. "Why did you do that?"

Michael dropped his hands, rolling his tongue over the roof of his mouth. "Because I like to French kiss."

She shook her head, her hair fanning over her breasts. "No, I mean, why did you kiss me at all?"

He plowed both hands through his hair. "God knows. I must be nuts."

"You weren't," she said, her soft voice carrying a dangerous undercurrent, "perhaps trying to distract me from our conversation, were you?"

His hands stilled on his head. "I don't even know what we were talking about anymore."

"You letting it slip about who my father is?"

"I told you—" Michael swallowed his retort. The crazy woman had just bitten his damn tongue. He wasn't about to stand here and plead for her to believe him. "If you'll excuse me, Ms. Welham, I believe I'll go suck on some ice cubes."

3

WORD SPREAD faster than wildfire who Darcy really was. She had no doubts about the source of the news. As her co-workers discovered her identity, they withdrew from her as if she'd caught a case of the plague.

It hurt. People had always given Darcy a wide berth, whether it had been her schoolmates or the ladies hired to care for her while her parents worked such long hours trying to establish their business.

She'd learned to live with it. She understood why people considered her bad luck, even if she didn't feel she'd entirely earned her reputation. But here, the other workers had for a while cheerfully accepted her into the fold. And then the rat had gone and ruined it for her.

She sat all alone in the break room. As soon as she'd entered, the others had silently gotten up and left. More than ever in her life, she felt isolated and lonely.

A tear slipped from her eye. And then another, and another. Her shoulders shook with the effort to stop the flow. She *never* cried. Never. Crying was for people who allowed themselves to feel the hurt. She'd spent a lifetime fighting that weakness.

Darcy pulled a hanky from her apron and blew her nose. She couldn't let Michael Davidson see her cowed. She wouldn't.

"Darcy, you have another table—what's wrong?"

Darcy looked up through a blur of tears. Anthony stood in the doorway, looking helpless.

She gave him a shaky smile. "Nothing. I'm fine."

"Like hell," he said gruffly, patting her shoulder. "What's the matter?"

His kindness was the last straw. Before she could stop herself, she was blurting out the entire story. "I'm not trying to hurt anyone, Anthony! I...I just want to keep the only thing left of m-my m-mother's. I swear, if I can convince my father to let me run the business, I'll match all of the benefits that s-stupid company is offering."

"Sure you will, kid."

Darcy swatted the moisture from her face and looked up. That's when she realized that several of the employees had joined them. Anthony glared down every single one of them. One by one, their expressions became slightly shamefaced. Then, amazingly, they looked at her differently. Kindly. Compassionately.

"I swear it!" she repeated for good measure. "You'll be better off with me."

Slowly they each smiled at her. Darcy wanted to cry again, only this time out of pure joy.

Tom appeared in the doorway, and the chatter came to a screeching halt. "What the hell is this, a convention?"

Everyone scrambled to leave, but Tom stopped them. "Actually, I'm glad you're all here." He looked at Darcy with sympathy.

Her stomach fluttered. "What is it?" she whispered.

"Your father's here, Darce."

She jumped up, smiling. "Daddy's here? Where?"

"Seated in your section."

"Oh, no! Tom, how could you?"

"It wasn't my fault. Davidson must have arranged it."

"Davidson?" she squeaked, dread a palpable thing inside her.

"They're having dinner together."

"That rat!" Darcy cried. "That dirty, rotten, no-good, slimy snake. He's doing this on purpose. He's going to try to show my father that I can't even handle a simple meal. I'll kill him!"

"Now, Darcy, calm down," Tom said. "You know what happens when you get upset."

"No. What?"

He waved. "Never mind. Listen, we'll all help you. Won't we, folks?" he asked, staring down everyone in the room. One by one, bless them, they nodded.

Tom grinned. "Good." He grasped Darcy's shoulders. "Take a deep breath and go get 'em, tiger."

MICHAEL WATCHED Darcy approach and he mentally rubbed his hands together. This was a stroke of pure luck, and he didn't want to miss a minute of it. When Darcy's father had contacted Michael and invited him to dinner, Michael had agreed in a heartbeat. But he'd had no idea the man had called ahead and specified seating in his daughter's section. One look at Darcy waiting tables and Edward Welham would probably sign the papers tonight.

Michael realized he was risking his life for the sake of his company, but it was a risk worth taking. His boss had all but told him that he needed this acquisition to secure his new position. He could almost picture his diplomas hanging on the wall of that plush, large, corner office.

But more than that office, he wanted to see the pride in his mother's eyes when she learned about the promotion. And he wanted to shove his business card with his new title down his damned grandfather's throat.

He closed his eyes, swallowing the anger. And the guilt. And the overwhelming need to prove that his birth wasn't a mistake.

Opening his eyes, he glared at Darcy, the one woman standing between him and his ultimate goal. For a total klutz, she sure had a graceful air about her. Too bad she was the enemy. He didn't relish making a fool of her in front of her father. But business was business. He hadn't gotten to his position by letting a pair of kissable lips and great breasts distract him.

Michael's face went warm when he realized he'd been thinking about that kiss too often in the last two days. And nights. Edward Welham was a little rough around the edges, but all in all Michael respected him a great deal. Michael didn't think the man would appreciate his prurient thoughts.

Ed Welham had a very distinguished air, his teak-brown hair going gray only at the temples, and his deep green eyes stamping proof of his relationship to his daughter upon him. Yet, Ed's eyes gleamed with shrewd business sense. His daughter's sparkled with something else. Something Michael didn't want to decipher.

"Hello, gentlemen," Darcy said, all business. "I'm Darcy, and I'll be taking care of you this evening."

With a promise like that coming from Darcy, Michael wondered if he shouldn't have paramedics standing by.

Her father chuckled. "Ah, Princess, cut the crap."

Princess? Yup, figures he'd call her Princess.

Darcy darted a look both ways, then quickly bent and pressed a kiss on her father's cheek. "Hi, Daddy."

Edward patted her hand, gazing up at her fondly. "Staying out of trouble, Princess?"

Michael almost snorted. Darcy's narrowed gaze stopped him. She returned her attention to her father. "I'm having fun, Daddy."

Touché, Michael thought. That was probably the best non-answer he'd ever heard. Of course, she probably had a lot of practice.

"Darcy, who burned down the house?"

"Want to roast some wienies, Daddy?"

Straightening to almost military stiffness, she said, "Now, what can I get you two from the bar?"

They ordered cocktails, then, as Darcy walked away without a single mishap in round one, Michael watched Edward watch his daughter. His eyes glowed with a father's pride. That told Michael he needed to tread carefully. He didn't want to offend the man by insulting his daughter.

Edward dragged his attention away from Darcy. "She blow anything up yet?" he asked, grinning.

Michael's mouth almost dropped open. He stared mutely at the man.

Laughing, Edward said, "Don't worry, Davidson. I know all about my daughter's…hmm…accident-prone nature." He sighed. "Her mother and I used to believe that Darcy's exploits were a way of getting attention, because we were gone so much. But as she grew up and didn't grow out of it, we were forced to face facts."

Michael sat forward. "With all due respect, sir, a restaurant is a dangerous place for someone with your daughter's…nature."

"This is true. Which was why we always thought it best to keep her away when she was younger. We were just too busy to supervise her." He looked at his hand thoughtfully. "I'm not certain that wasn't a mistake."

"I'm sure you did what you thought best," Michael said. But he wondered about that. The restaurant business kept crazy hours, especially for an owner. Who'd watched Darcy while her parents built an empire?

He shook his head. What did he care who'd baby-sat the woman? As far as he was concerned, she still needed a keeper, if for nothing else than to save her from killing herself or someone else.

Leaning on his crossed forearms, he asked, "If Darcy didn't have anything to do with the restaurants growing up, why her sudden interest in keeping them now?"

"Got me by the tail. I was as surprised as anyone when she came flying home in a huff. I'd had no idea she was so sentimental about the restaurants." His lips pursed. "To tell you the truth, I lost all sentiment for the restaurants the moment Jeannie died. I only kept them this long to give me something to keep me busy." He grinned. "But I'm at that age where a round of golf a day is all the busy I need."

Their drinks arrived, and Michael braced himself to get his poured in his lap. When she deposited them without incident, he frowned.

Darcy shot him a triumphant, haughty look, then gave full attention to her father. "The specials tonight are trout amandine, broiled prawns and veal marsala. The soups are black bean and cream of broccoli, and the vegetable is steamed zucchini. Ready to order, or do you want a few minutes?''

Edward arched a brow at Michael. Michael waved, fully prepared to get this show on the road and take whatever punishment she could dish out.

Without opening his menu, Edward said, ''I'll start with the escargot, broccoli soup and the prime rib. Rare. Big cut.''

Darcy nodded. ''No appetizer, house salad with the raspberry vinaigrette and the trout.''

''Aw, Princess,'' Edward complained. ''Relax, will ya?''

''Your arteries will thank me someday.''

''But this is a celebration!''

Her gaze snapped up and she took a step backward, nearly slamming into a customer. ''A celebration? What kind of celebration?''

Michael crossed his fingers under the table.

Edward lifted his highball glass in toast. ''Why, celebrating seeing my little girl working in one of my restaurants, of course.''

She looked like she wanted to puddle to the floor in relief. Her laughter shook. ''Oh, Daddy!''

Michael uncrossed his fingers and mentally listed his seven favorite foul words.

Darcy turned her attention to him, and her eyes grew cool. ''And you?'' she asked crisply.

Snapping the menu closed, he said, ''Salad, house dressing and prime rib. Rare. Baked potato. Sour cream.''

She nodded without protest, apparently not concerned about *his* arteries.

Michael noted, not for the first time, that Darcy didn't bother writing down their order. Once, he'd even seen her take an order for a party of fifteen without ever jotting down a word. He'd inquired later how badly she'd messed up that table's order, only to find out she'd gotten it exactly right. The woman had to have the memory of an elephant.

The grace of a bull and the memory of an elephant. The grace of a bull, the memory of an elephant and the face of a goddess.

Michael shook his head.

Taking their menus, Darcy turned...and nearly toppled a waiter, laden with a large tray of food. He sidestepped her deftly. "Sorry, Darcy, I didn't see you."

Michael's eyes narrowed on the young man. Apologizing to Darcy, for nearly knocking him over? Well, she'd avoided two disasters so far, but he knew she couldn't last the night. She just couldn't.

As soon as she was gone, he said, "In truth, Edward, there have been several costly accidents lately. I think you'll probably find that the profits for this restaurant will have diminished significantly over the last month."

"I suspected as much."

Michael didn't know what else to say on that topic, so he changed the subject back to golf—Edward's passion, and Michael's hobby.

A short time later, Darcy returned. Anthony carried her tray of salads, which confirmed Michael's suspicions that there was a conspiracy going on here to keep Darcy from embarrassing herself. Michael supposed he should be irritated, but for some reason the thought warmed him a little. Apparently the other employees had forgiven Darcy for being a Welham. Considering how upset she'd been the other day, he felt a strange gladness.

Darcy passed out the salads without mishap. She looked so pleased with herself, Michael felt his business edge dull just a little.

"Pepper?"

He blinked. "Hmm?"

She waved a large pepper mill in front of him. "Would you like some freshly ground pepper?"

"Oh, yeah, sure."

She began grinding pepper onto his salad...right near his nose.

Michael tried to sit back, but that pepper mill trailed after him like a magnet. "Enough," he said, twitching his nose to get rid of the tickle.

Grind. Grind. Grind.

"Thank you, that's e-e-e-ah-*choo!*"

She stopped grinding. "More?"

His warm, fuzzy feelings vanished as he saw the humorous gleam in her eye. Shielding his salad with his hands, he said mildly, "No, thank you," all the while plotting revenge.

She moved to her father and gave him three small twists of pepper, then sashayed away, obviously proud of herself.

Edward dug into his salad with relish. Michael looked at his own. The lettuce, popcorn shrimp and creamy garlic dressing were all coated with enough pepper to season a side of beef. He tried to push the pepper to one side and dig underneath for some virgin lettuce. He took a bite. Swallowing, he grabbed for his water and drained half the glass.

Putting aside his salad fork, he looked around the restaurant for Darcy. The little tart.

A deafening crash from the kitchen rattled the windows in the dining room. Michael shot to his feet. "Come on. I'm sure your daughter will be in the vicinity of the latest disaster."

Edward followed him into the kitchen.

Chaos reigned. Anthony was trying to clean up what looked like the remains of six or seven dinner servings while waiters and waitresses jumped over him. The chef was swearing in Italian and shaking a spatula at the waste of food. Tom was trying to hand salads, condiments, coffee, whatever, to people who yelled for help.

Darcy wasn't there.

Michael almost growled. He had no doubt Darcy was behind the latest mishap. Somehow, someway, she'd caused this situation. "Where's Darcy?" he asked Tom.

Tom raised innocent brows. "Darcy?"

"How'd this happen?" Michael demanded.

Just then one of the waiters stopped and turned. "I'm sorry, Tom. I'll be more careful next time."

"You do that," Tom said gruffly. He nodded at Edward. "I've got this under control. Go on out and enjoy the rest of your meal."

Michael felt the bite of frustration. Shaking his head, he followed Edward back out to the dining room.

Tom waited several heartbeats after the two men left the kitchen. Then he ambled over to the freezer. Peeking in, he caught Darcy biting her thumbnail. "You can come out now. They're gone."

MICHAEL COULDN'T BELIEVE this night. Darcy had done everything right, or, if she hadn't, she and the other employees were covering her mistakes nicely. He'd subtly tried to shake her up, but so far hadn't had any success. Instead, she'd peppered his salad and sprinkled just enough lemon juice on his prime rib to ruin the flavor and set his still tender tongue on fire.

He couldn't wait to see what she did to his pie.

He watched her nearly gut Anthony, then drop the knife in horror. He started to tell on her, but something stopped him. No doubt about it, the lady was dangerous. And yet, there was something so vulnerable about her, he almost felt sorry for her.

"Tell me about Darcy," he said, then blinked in surprise, wondering where that had come from.

Edward took a sip of wine before answering him. "What about her?"

"Is she your only child?"

"Yes, she is." Edward smiled, a little sadly, Michael thought. "Jeannie and I were only blessed once, unfortunately. But we did a good job that one time, just the same."

Physically, Michael couldn't argue the point. Darcy Welham was one stunning lady. Unfortunately, plenty of nature's disasters had a haunting beauty. He looked over at her thoughtfully. She was still talking to the busboy, who'd picked up the knife and started cutting the pie for her.

When he'd first learned that the acquisition had ground to a halt because the owner's daughter had stamped her pampered foot and put a stop to it, Michael had been furious. In fact, he was still furious. Unfortunately, she didn't quite fit the image he'd conjured up of her. Darcy didn't remind him of a spoiled little daddy's girl. But that was exactly what she was.

Wasn't she?

Yes, of course she was. He didn't care that she seemed to work as hard or harder than the other staff. He didn't care that she hadn't lorded who she was over the other employees—had, in fact, wanted to remain anonymous. He didn't care that she drove a battered Chevy when he knew for a fact that she could afford any luxury sports car her little heart desired. She was still Darcy Welham, the woman who stood in his way.

Michael didn't let anything stand in his way. Especially when so much was at stake. His grandfather's only words to him rang through Michael's mind. *Garbage in, garbage out.* He hadn't understood what his grandfather had meant, the first time he'd heard him say it.

Michael had been ten. He'd just returned from delivering papers on a slushy winter morning. He'd walked into the apartment, frozen and muddy, to find a man he'd never seen before standing in their tiny living room, looking huge and nasty.

Michael had immediately moved to stand in front of his mother, glaring up at the menacing man. The man had glared right back. Then shaking his head, he'd muttered, "Garbage in, garbage out," stuffed his hands into leather gloves, and stalked out of their home.

That had been his first and only meeting with his maternal grandfather. It wasn't until a few years later, in a computer-science class, that he'd heard the words spoken again and finally understood their meaning.

His grandfather didn't know it, but he'd been inadvertently responsible for what drove Michael to succeed at all costs. One day Michael would confront the son of a bitch.

He wanted the man to know just what kind of "garbage" Michael's mother had produced.

Michael shook his head.

Darcy looked over at their table, and in his newly revived fury, Michael waved her over. She went a little stiff, glaring at him from across the room. Standing frozen for several seconds, she seemed to be contemplating her next move. Then she did something that made Michael suck in his breath.

She touched her fingers to her lips.

Blood roared through his ears, then rushed straight to his groin, the memory of that kiss so fresh he could almost feel the pressure of her lips even now. And suddenly he knew he wanted to kiss her again.

God, he was in trouble.

"Darcy had a tough time of it, growing up," Michael heard through the buzzing in his head.

"What?" he croaked, dragging his gaze from her.

Ed Welham nodded. "She did."

"How so?" Michael asked, more interested than he should have been.

Ed wiped his lips with his napkin, then tossed it on the table with a sigh. "Growing up, she was painfully shy. She had very few friends. And the poor young thing was all legs."

Michael thought most women would kill to be "all legs," but kept his opinion to himself.

"Jeannie and I were gone for long stretches of time," Ed said, seeming lost in thought. "We needed someone home full-time to watch Darcy. Unfortunately, her mishaps tended to drive nannies away. And the more nannies who left her, the more her self-esteem suffered." Ed sighed. "We tried to make up for it, but weren't always successful."

Taking a breath, Michael shoved aside the sympathy that welled inside him. It wouldn't do to soften toward the enemy. Before he knew it, he'd be ripping up the takeover papers in front of the woman, and waltzing away, giving her the company, and him a possible demotion.

No, he had to put a lock on these thoughts, these feelings. It wasn't like he was yanking her childhood blanket or teddy bear from her. They were just restaurants, for God's sake! You couldn't hug the restaurants, couldn't let them comfort you in return.

Irritated, Michael waved at a dawdling Darcy again.

Frowning, she marched over to the table, a plate of pie in each hand. Dumping them on the table, she glared at Michael. "Anything else?"

"A smile might be nice," Michael said dryly.

"Not on the menu. Do you want anything else or not? You're not my only customers, you know."

"I'll take some coffee, Princess."

Darcy's expression softened. "Decaf coming up."

Ed rolled his eyes. "Fine."

Michael almost liked Ed enough to warn him that wasn't a good idea. But this was his last chance to show Edward how wrong this environment was for her. He prayed no permanent damage was done to either of them. "I'll take some, too."

Her smile vanished as she nodded curtly. "By the way, if you'd have had to pay for this meal, it would have cost you—" she closed her eyes, her mouth moving silently "—seventy-five dollars and twenty-eight cents. Twenty percent of that is...fifteen dollars and six cents." She slapped a small black tray on the table. "You can leave the tip here." She walked away.

Michael stared at the tray, then looked up at Ed. "How'd she do that? She didn't even ring it up?"

Waving, Ed said, "She's pretty good with numbers."

"Does she have a calculator in her head or something?"

"One of her favorite games growing up was to have Jeannie and me rattle off numbers at her. As fast as we could say them, Darcy could add, subtract, multiply and divide. When she was thirteen years old, she corrected my tax return. Probably saved me from an audit."

Michael shook his head. This was the woman he'd thought of as a ditz?

Ed smiled at him. "You might do well to change tactics, you know."

"Excuse me, sir?"

"You might try a little charm. Get her to like you. Then maybe she'll listen a little more reasonably to your offer."

"Why would she have to listen to our offer?" Michael asked, dreading the answer.

Edward didn't surprise him. "Because much as I'm anxious for this deal to go through, to begin my retirement, I'm not signing one page until Darcy gives the word." He took a bite of pie while Michael silently fumed. After a sip of water, Edward added, "Switch tactics, Davidson. You'll never change Darcy's mind by antagonizing her. She's stubborn like her mama that way."

Michael closed his eyes and thought his options through. He apparently didn't have any. The key—the only key—to acquiring Welham's was through Darcy. Opening his eyes, he smiled grimly. "Have any suggestions?"

Ed shrugged. "Darcy's used to people running away from her before they really get to know her. Can't imagine how she'd react to someone wanting to know her. Really know her. I honestly don't think the restaurant business holds that much interest for her. I honestly think in the back of Darcy's mind, she has other goals and dreams. Maybe you could get to know her and learn what those goals are."

Michael swallowed again, and pushed away his pie. Getting to know Darcy sounded dangerous to him.

Extremely dangerous.

He rolled his sore tongue around his mouth. Physically hazardous.

His mind conjured up the image of Darcy's dazed gaze as he'd kissed her. Emotionally lethal.

A sense of dread sank through him. The battle lines were clearly drawn, but Michael realized his tactics needed some revising. Glancing at Darcy's father, he waved weakly. "Get to know her. Right."

4

It DIDN'T TAKE a genius to know Michael had a daunting task ahead of him. Considering the way he and Darcy had started out, he almost needed a miracle. He'd spent a restless night, listing his options. And the very next day he started working on them.

He waited until Darcy entered Welham's back kitchen before popping a forkful of coconut cheesecake into his mouth.

"Mmmm," he moaned, closing his eyes. "Delicious."

He took another bite, then addressed his comment to one of the assistant chefs. "Whoever created this recipe is gifted!"

"Hope you choke on it, Davidson," Darcy said under her breath as she passed behind him.

He gritted his teeth, pretending he hadn't heard her. As soon as she clocked in and left, he shoved the half-eaten pie at the dishwasher. Picking up his clipboard, he slapped at the pages of his legal pad until he came to the page titled *The Darcy Dilemma*.

Sweeping his gaze down the list, he came to item number three: *Try flattery*. He crossed it out with a vengeance, then wrote beside it, *Flattery won't work*.

Two days later, Michael strolled up to Darcy as she punched in an order on the computerized terminal. He eavesdropped on her mumbling.

"The man with the red hair…potato soup, stuffed shrimp, side of spaghetti and a coke…"

Forcing a friendly smile on his face, he said, "Hey, you're doing a great job with that party of ten."

She looked up quickly. And promptly rang up about a thousand dollars' worth of food. "Oh, no! Now look what you made me do!"

"Hey, don't worry," he said, his voice as soothing as possible. He reached over and pressed the cancel button, breathing in her alluring perfume. "There. All gone."

She turned to him and rested her hip against the counter. Crossing her arms over her chest, she managed to turn glaring into an art form. "All gone, all right. Every single item I just keyed in for that party of ten I'm doing such a bang-up job on."

Michael shot her a sheepish grimace. "Sorry."

"What are you up to, Davidson?"

"Up to?"

"I'm not buying this sudden friendliness, so you might as well give it up." With that she turned back to the computer and started jabbing in her orders, muttering what sounded suspiciously like a list of names. None of them nice.

A whole slew of retorts bounced through Michael's mind. Before he could choose just which one he wanted to fling at her, she pushed him aside and sailed into the kitchen.

Swearing under his breath, he went to Tom's office and grabbed his clipboard.

He crossed out item number two, *Try acting friendly.* Beside it he wrote, *Friendliness isn't working.*

"YOUR HAIR looks very pretty tonight," Michael told Darcy later that night. She'd taken it down after her shift was over, and he'd walked into the break room as she combed it out.

It wasn't a lie. Michael could spend a few weeks getting lost in that hair. He'd never known he'd particularly had a hair fetish, but after seeing Darcy's, he was certain that thick, long, silky hair was a feature he wanted the women he dated to possess.

His compliment fell on deaf ears. Darcy ignored him,

flinging her hair over her head and bending over, to comb it from her nape to the ends.

"I bet a lot of the men you dated loved your hair," he said, trying again.

Her brush stilled in midstroke. Since her hair completely obliterated her face, he couldn't see her expression.

He itched to rub some of the strands through his fingers, but he thought that might be taking his flirtation a little too far. So he settled for verbal assaults. "Has anyone ever told you you look like Grace Kelly?"

That got her attention. She swiped the brush through her hair one last time, then flung the blond mass back over her head. She didn't appear all that flattered.

"No," she replied tersely.

"I think the resemblance is uncanny."

"Too bad you don't look a thing like Cary Grant," she retorted, then moved to walk by him.

Frustrated, Michael grasped her arm. "Why do you dislike me so much, Darcy?" he asked, surprised that it really bothered him. "I know we got off to a bad start, but I'm really trying here. Can't you meet me halfway?"

She pulled her arm from his grasp. "Why?" she asked suspiciously. "Why this sudden interest in me?"

His eyes traveled lazily over her features, and he gave her what he hoped was a slow, provocative smile. "You're a damn beautiful woman. Surely you're aware of that."

Her snort wasn't exactly the type one expected to hear from a beautiful Grace Kelly type. "May I recommend *To Catch a Thief*? Cary was particularly charming in that one."

Michael hissed one short, succinct swearword while he watched Darcy stroll away. *Flirting sure isn't working,* he thought, following her.

"CAN I HELP you with that?"

Startled by the deep voice behind her, Darcy jumped...and promptly lost her balance on the stool. Her arms flapped like a bird's as she tried to keep from falling.

She lost the battle with gravity.

And fell right into Michael Davidson's arms.

He looked as startled to find her there as she herself felt. His arms were steel bands under her body. If holding her was a strain, it didn't show in his face. In fact, his surprise had faded and another look took its place, one that made her flush with heat. His eyes fastened on her lips, giving Darcy no doubt about where his thoughts had strayed.

With what looked like effort, he dragged his gaze up to stare into her eyes. "You all right?"

No, she was not all right. She was far from all right. In fact, she'd lay odds she was slightly out of her mind at the moment. She had this awful desire to put her arms around his neck and lay her head on his shoulder.

Probably because a man had never held her like this. Or maybe because his aftershave smelled wonderful. Or possibly because he was about the best-looking man she'd ever seen. Whatever—she felt a little too comfortable in the enemy's arms.

She wiggled. "Put me down."

He did, nearly dumping her on her rump.

Darcy automatically clutched his arm, trying to steady herself. His muscles flexed under her fingers. She stared at his arm in surprise. No wonder he'd had no trouble holding her. That was one big muscle under there.

She looked up and caught his amused smile. Snatching her hand back, she hiked her chin. "Thanks for almost getting me killed."

His amusement vanished. "Almost killing you! I just saved your tail, woman!"

"I wouldn't have fallen if you hadn't snuck up behind me."

"I was trying to help!"

Darcy glared at the man. A week had passed since his dinner with her father. Over the course of those days, Michael Davidson had continued to stick to her like a shadow, but something had changed, something subtle. He no longer looked at her as if she were a social disease. He no longer took notes whenever Darcy made a mistake. He'd even taken down the breakage chart.

The creep was up to something.

"If I want your help, I'll ask for it," she retorted. "And believe me, I won't."

The creep-who-was-up-to-something stared at her, then slowly shook his head. As he walked away, she thought he mumbled something about charm and brick walls.

MICHAEL CONSIDERED himself an intelligent man. Resourceful. Organized. Even creative when he had to be.

But as he looked down at the page on his legal pad, frustration clouded his mind. The Darcy Dilemma was driving him crazy. Over the week since his dinner with Ed Welham, he'd tried to subtly act kinder to her. He'd even tried to tease her a little. She'd responded to all of his efforts with suspicion.

He glared at his list.

Charm isn't working, he'd written. Boy, now there was an understatement. Darcy Welham wouldn't recognize charm if it came up and bit her on the butt.

He had to admit, he didn't think Darcy had much practice with men. Whenever he'd tried to tease her, she seemed to digest the gesture, analyze it, looking for hidden meaning. He suspected she wasn't used to men flirting with her.

Flirting isn't working.

Friendliness isn't working. Another understatement.

What the hell was he going to do with the woman? How would he ever get her to listen rationally to Dining Incorporated's offer? The only time she'd acted positively toward him was...when he'd kissed her.

Kissing her worked, he scribbled.

Michael stared at the words, his mind racing furiously. No, he couldn't even *think* about it. He was a businessman. He kept his personal life completely separate and distinct from his professional life. The two didn't belong in the same universe, much less the world.

Besides, although he found Darcy attractive, he didn't

much like her. He'd never been drawn to the innocent type. He liked his women aggressive and open, free of sexual inhibitions. He liked the type who knew what they wanted, and went after it. And he definitely preferred women who had at least *some* experience with men.

He'd bet his life savings that Darcy Welham was a virgin. Michael didn't do virgins. He'd seen too many of his buddies take their share of virgins, and soon found the women draped around their necks. Apparently, women took the gift of their virginity much more seriously than men did. Michael didn't have the time or inclination for serious commitments. He had goals to accomplish, and he couldn't do that if he had a woman in his life distracting him.

He shook his head. What the hell was he thinking about? How had he made the leap from kissing Darcy to making love to her? He had no intention of making love with the woman. God, kissing her had nearly lost him a tongue. He shuddered to think what would happen to the rest of his exposed body if he gave her a shot at it.

Besides, he did have a conscience. Seducing Ms. Welham in order to soften her seemed morally…wrong. Professionally unethical. Psychologically cruel.

But physically…damn appealing.

He looked down at his legal pad again and swore softly. *Kissing her worked.*

Technically, kissing a woman didn't necessarily constitute seducing her. As long as he kept himself under control, didn't allow it to progress to anything more intimate, maybe a kiss or two would do the trick. Maybe she'd stop thinking of him as a monster trying to take her dream away from her. Maybe it could soften her just enough that she'd listen to reason.

He underlined the words for emphasis. Then his precise, orderly brain began to plan.

Get her alone.

Show her appreciation.

Kiss her.

Michael took a deep breath, trying to deny his body its

instinctive reaction to the thought. With an effort of will, he wrestled back control of his hormones. He was doing this strictly for the sake of his company. He had to keep that in mind at all costs. With that final instruction to himself, he wrote one last item.

Keep your damn tongue out of her mouth.

MICHAEL STROLLED through the men's locker room of Alexandria's health club and walked into the indoor Olympic pool area. The air was heavy with humidity and the scent of chlorine.

Glancing around, he tried to locate Darcy.

Not an hour after he'd made up his mind about his new plan of attack, he'd heard one of the other waitresses ask Darcy how she stayed so thin. Darcy had mentioned that she swam laps at this club five nights a week.

That news had surprised Michael. Somehow he hadn't pictured Darcy as the swimmer type. In fact, he'd have laid odds that Darcy could manage to drown herself standing in a puddle of water.

He looked in turn at each of the three people in the pool, all swimming laps. Two were women, both swimming freestyle, both with white caps on their heads.

Disappointment sluiced through him. Neither of them was Darcy, he knew, without seeing their faces. One was far too short, and the other was far too graceful.

The graceful one performed a perfect flip at the near end of the pool, then glided several yards under the water. When she began swimming, she switched smoothly into a breaststroke.

Michael took the time to appreciate her long legs, and the curve of her bottom beneath a navy Speedo suit. If her face came close to looking as good as her legs, he might just have to introduce himself.

When she reached the deep end, the woman pulled herself from the pool in one fluid movement. Michael nearly swallowed his tongue. With a body like that, it wouldn't matter if she looked like the Wicked Witch of the West.

Heedless of his gaping attention, the lady pulled goggles from her eyes, then the cap from her head. Shaking out her hair—her long, long, blond hair—she strolled to a bench and grabbed a bottle of Evian water.

Darcy.

Michael's knees suddenly went weak as his gaze traced every curve on her slick body. God Almighty, the woman was breathtaking. She had delicate shoulders and long, lean thighs, a flat abdomen and anything-but-flat breasts. She had a woman's body that called out to him to touch, explore, possess.

He stepped back into the locker room, taking deep, calming breaths. His body had never reacted so strongly to the sight of a woman since the first time he'd had sex. He appreciated the feminine form as much—if not more—than the rest of mankind, but this was the first time he felt like he'd been hit by a tornado of raging hormones. He felt on fire.

And he was supposed to stop at just kissing her?

Deep inside of him, Michael knew he should switch tactics *instantly,* should drop this plan to ply Darcy with a few kisses. Deep inside, he knew that the stakes had just gone up, and he had much more to lose by kissing her than he'd ever gain by getting her to agree to D.I.'s offer. Deep down inside, he knew the smartest thing he could do was take the first shuttle back to New York and forget about the Welham's restaurant chain and the owner's daughter.

Apparently his brain didn't reach that deep.

This is business, Davidson, he tried to tell himself. Unfortunately, he felt distinctly unbusinesslike. Unfortunately, he felt distinctly personal-like. He could almost see his clearly defined goals melt and change form, become fuzzy and warm. He needed to get away and think.

Instead of getting away, he stepped back into the pool room. Darcy wasn't doing laps any longer. Instead, damn her, she was poised on what looked like about a five-meter-high diving platform.

His jaw dropped as she hurled herself into the air, then

as if in slow motion he watched her do a one-and-a-half flip with a twist, knifing straight into the water arms and head first.

When she surfaced, an angelic smile on her face, Michael released his breath, just realizing he'd been holding it. In a fog of confusion, he watched her swim lazily to the ladder.

"Amazing, isn't she?"

Michael's head snapped around at the sound of the man's voice. The guy who'd been swimming laps earlier stood beside him, a towel draped around his neck.

Michael didn't much care for the man's opinion of Darcy. He also didn't like the way the guy's eyes followed Darcy's movements as she returned to the platform. "Yes, she is."

The man chuckled. "Let me give you fair warning. The package might be entertaining, but if you get too close, you're asking for trouble."

"What do you mean?"

"I mean, the lady may look good in a pool, but she's big trouble in the real world."

No matter that Michael agreed completely with the man, he took offense on Darcy's behalf. "What do you mean by trouble?"

"She's a jinx."

"Excuse me?"

"Exactly three guys have approached her to try to ask her out. Two ended up getting stitches, one was a little luckier...just a slight concussion."

"She attacked them?"

"That's the problem. She didn't mean to hurt them. Like I said, she's trouble."

Michael winced. "I don't think I want to know the details."

"Just trying to help," the stranger said. "If you know what's good for you, keep a safe distance." The man turned and disappeared into the locker room.

Michael had always prided himself on knowing what was

good for him. Since the time he'd been five years old he'd been setting goals, then making lists on the plans of action that would win him those goals. He'd found his method highly successful so far.

So why, when he knew that continuing his plan to win Darcy over could land him in big trouble, wasn't he running like a madman from this health club?

As he watched Darcy execute a perfect jackknife, he knew he had his answer. Because the only thing between his ears right now was the knowledge of what Darcy Welham looked like in a bathing suit.

Shaking his head, he dropped his towel on the wooden bench, kicked off his docksiders and pulled his T-shirt over his head, leaving himself clad only in a pair of swimming trunks with the insignia of his alma mater, Columbia University, on it.

Darcy still hadn't noticed him.

The shorter woman had left. They were all alone in the pool. Item number one on his list had just been accomplished.

He walked to the pool's lip, rotating his arms to warm up his muscles. Gazing up, he watched Darcy set up for another dive. She raised her arms—over her head this time. Then she brought them down, bent her knees slightly, and prepared to shove off from the platform.

That's when she finally spotted Michael.

Even from across the pool he saw her eyes go wide, her mouth form an "oh!" of recognition. She tried to pull back, but momentum prevented her. Her arms and legs flailed almost comically as she tried to right herself in the air. She almost made it. But not quite.

If she'd been in a cannonball-splash competition, she'd have won.

Michael tensed, the moments before she surfaced seeming like hours. When she finally got her head above water, she looked a little like Cousin It. Her hair covered her face. She dunked back down and let the water push it back, then reappeared, treading water.

She didn't exactly look thrilled to see him.

"You!" she squealed.

Michael tried to appear surprised. "Darcy! Is that you?" Before she could answer, he sliced through the air and dove into the pool. Using a lazy breaststroke, he cut across the pool toward her, smiling at her. She glared at him the entire time, her hair floating around her.

He stopped in front of her and shook his hair out of his eyes. Treading water with his legs alone, he said, "Wow, this is a nice surprise."

"You mean a nightmare."

He ignored that. "I didn't know you swam."

"Why should you?"

He ignored that, too. "You're a terrific diver."

Her cheeks blushed a little. "Uh…thank you." She tucked her hair behind her ear. "Well, I guess I'm tired of swim—"

Michael reached out and wrapped his hand around her arm. Even that slight contact managed to shoot sparks through his nervous system. "Don't go."

She stared down at her arm, then looked back at him. He could tell by the green light in her eyes and the parting of her lips that she felt the same sensation he did from the wet skin-on-skin contact.

Michael was almost surprised they weren't electrocuted.

Some primitive impulse took his brain hostage. He widened the circumference of his undulating legs just enough to brush against hers. His eyes slid shut and he bit back a moan as he felt her silky-smooth skin.

Darcy gasped as she felt Michael Davidson's leg brush against hers. Something started quaking inside her. She suddenly felt as heavy as a lead weight and as light as a feather. She didn't know if she was going to sink or float.

The man was *touching* her. While he was touching her, he was *gazing* at her with eyes so blue, it almost hurt to look into them. Water dripped down from his hair, the drops tracing the contours of his proud cheeks, his strong jaw. His lips, turned up in a slight smile, seemed hard and sexy all at once.

God, this gorgeous enemy of a man was *touching* her.

Deciding she was definitely going to sink, Darcy started churning her legs just a little more frantically. She tried to say something, but words stuck in her throat, just scant inches above where her heart had started threatening to spar with her ribs.

"Stay," he coaxed, his voice a little throaty. "I want to watch you swim some more. I want to watch you dive."

He wanted to *watch* her. As far as she knew, she'd never had a man want to watch her before.

And this man who wanted to *watch* her was still *touching* her.

She suddenly became aware that he was pulling her through the water toward him. Her legs churned just a little harder, in rhythm with her churning tummy.

He brought her to within a few inches of him, until her breasts brushed his chest every once in a while. Darcy tried hard to remember that this man was her enemy, but as the two of them bobbed in the water, as her breasts came in occasional contact with his bare, hard chest, Darcy couldn't think of anything, except that she wanted to touch Michael Davidson too.

The hand that wasn't holding her arm came up and played with her hair in the water. He seemed to like to do that, swirling it around as if it were his paintbrush, and he was creating a masterpiece in chlorine.

He looked up at her, and Darcy's legs slowed as a languorous feeling stole over her. They slowed even further when he brushed his fingers over her cheek, tucking her hair behind her ear.

"I want to kiss you again, Darcy."

Her legs went as limp as overcooked noodles.

She started to sink. He grasped her around the waist and treaded water for both of them.

"Please, let me kiss you."

The word "no" should have passed her lips. Unfortunately, just the feel of her breasts crushed against his chest rendered her speechless. She moaned, a sound that came out sounding suspiciously like "please."

Then his lips were on hers, wet and tasting like chlorine and man. Like *him*. She hadn't forgotten the taste of him, not in the nine days, three hours and about twenty-five minutes since the last time they'd done this. She hadn't forgotten the relentless pressure, both to her lips and her lower belly. She hadn't forgotten the pleasurable abrasion of her chin and cheeks, where his stubbled jaw rubbed against her skin.

What she *had* forgotten was that she didn't want a man's tongue in her mouth.

Unfortunately, he hadn't forgotten. His tongue didn't come near hers. And the more he nipped at her lips, the more he pressed against her and molded his mouth against hers, the more she wanted to taste his tongue.

She broke the kiss. "Please!" she whispered desperately.

"What, Darcy?" he asked softly, his hand skimming up and down her back rhythmically while he held them afloat.

Her eyelashes fluttered as she directed her gaze at his jaw. "Kiss me."

His chest rumbled against hers, managing to excite her. "What do you think I've been doing?"

"Kiss me right."

The rumbling stopped abruptly. "You want me to?"

"Yes."

"You won't bite me again, will you?"

"No."

"Promise?"

"Promise." She managed to look up at him. "I swear."

The blaze in his eyes, the tightening of his jaw made her take in a quick breath. He was *touching* her. He was *holding* her. And he was going to *French kiss* her. Darcy felt faint.

His lips lowered to hers. Darcy parted hers beneath his insistent touch. She felt his heart thundering against her chest, and a surge of feminine power rose through her. This affected him. *She* affected him.

His teeth nibbled on her lips. Then he made a groaning sound that hit her like a laser. His tongue plunged into her mouth. It was so good, the way the sensations rocketed through her. Her knee jerked up in reaction.

Right between his legs.

Darcy felt him pull back.

Heard a grunt.

Then felt him drop away from her, sinking into the water.

"Uh-oh."

5

"I'M SORRY!" Darcy cried after dragging Michael to the pool's surface. "I'm so, so, so, so, so sorry!"

Michael kept his eyes closed and groaned softly. He quite frankly liked having Darcy's arms around him, and he wasn't about to do anything to make her let him go any faster.

She puffed a little as she towed him to the shallow end of the pool. "I swear I didn't—" puff, puff "—do it on purpose!"

He groaned again, putting a little more oomph in it this time.

She stopped and rolled out from behind him, still cradling him to her. "Michael?" she whispered, touching her fingertips to his jaw. "Michael, please tell me you're all right."

As far as he knew, this was the first time Darcy had spoken his given name. It surprised him how much he liked hearing it on her lips. Forcing himself not to open his eyes to watch those lips as she whispered his name, he bit back an honest groan as her breasts pressed into his ribs. Mentally, he updated his list. *Guilt works.*

Her fingers probed his neck, and he realized she was searching for a pulse. He had the sinking feeling that if his pulse was pounding as hard as his heart, she'd have no trouble finding it.

"Please, please, please," she chanted softly. "Is he breathing?"

Michael held his breath.

Strands of her hair plastered themselves to his face. He

guessed she'd put her ear to his mouth to see if air was moving in and out of it.

She cupped the back of his head, stuck her fingers between his lips and pried them apart. Then she did something that nearly made his lungs explode. She sealed her lips over his mouth and blew with all her might.

Michael jerked in reaction, expelling all of that extra air. He got his legs under him and stood, still sputtering.

The fear in Darcy's eyes slowly turned to confusion, then was transformed into outrage. "You were faking!"

"Only a little."

"You weren't hurt at all!"

"Oh, yes I was," he insisted. After all, she'd nearly inflated him like a hot-air balloon.

The accusation in her eyes died. "Are you all right?" she asked softly.

"I think so."

Her lashes fluttered as she directed her attention to his groin. "I...it was an accident."

"I know."

"I...I don't know what...happened to me."

Michael plucked a wet strand of hair from her cheek, making certain to brush her skin with his fingertips. A surge of desire burst through him, confounding him. Why did he react so strongly to her?

So what if she was stunning, standing there wet and almost naked, her eyes glittering a deep, deep green? So what if her nipples strained against her suit, and her lips were moist and still slightly swollen from his kiss? So what if her nose was just slightly impudent, her cheekbones classic, her chin darlingly stubborn? So what if her thick, wheat-blond hair was slicked straight back from her forehead? He should be completely immune to her. He *wanted* to be completely immune to her. This was *business!*

So why did he want to be buried inside her so badly, he ached with it?

He traced circles on her shoulder. "What happened was, you felt the same thing I did from that kiss."

"I don't know what you mean," she said, glaring at his roaming fingers.

"You can't deny the attraction between us, Darcy. You'd be lying."

Her gaze skittered back to his face. "But I don't *want* to be attracted to you. You're my enemy."

"I don't have to be. We could be friends."

"Friends?" she squeaked, as if the word were foreign to her.

"Friends," he said softly. "And maybe lovers."

He hadn't known he was going to throw out that suggestion until it had already passed his lips. But once it came out, for some reason it felt right. Really right. In fact, suddenly it felt as imperative to him as oxygen.

She didn't agree with him, apparently. At least the shock on her face let him know the thought of him as a lover had never crossed her mind. Feeling a little insulted that she'd never viewed him as potential sex-partner material, he squeezed her shoulder.

"You wouldn't regret it, Darcy."

"Lo-lovers?" she whispered. "Are you saying what I think you're saying?"

God help him, yes. He wanted to get naked and sweaty with this woman. He wanted to explore the hidden delights her body held. He wanted her writhing under him. He wanted to make her explode with blissful release. And it had nothing at all to do with business, and everything to do with the wet lady before him.

For the first time in his life, Michael wondered if he had some sort of death wish.

He smiled gently. "What do you think I'm saying?"

"You...want to have sex with me?"

"Is that so hard to believe?"

"Yes."

He cupped her neck, his thumb caressing the sensitive skin under her ear. "Why?"

She sucked in a soft breath. "No one's ever wanted to before."

"Then the men in your life have either been blind or fools."

"There haven't been many," she admitted, her color rising. "I'm considered bad luck."

"Why?"

"I'm...not very graceful."

He fought the urge to nod his agreement. "Sweetheart, I just watched you swim and dive. You've got natural grace."

"In a pool, maybe."

"Well, then, while we're...together, just pretend you're in a pool."

Her lips pursed. "This is ridiculous. I've known you for a total of three weeks, and to tell you the truth, I haven't exactly liked you much."

If she'd been as graceful as she was blunt, she could have been a prima ballerina. "Well, how about if we take care of that part first?"

"What do you mean?"

"I'm a pretty decent guy, Darcy, no matter what you may think. Give me a chance to prove that to you. The rest will take care of itself."

"Why do you care what I think?"

He didn't know anymore, he realized with a jolt. Yes, he wanted to soften her so that she'd listen to reason. But he had a sinking feeling his determination to change Darcy's mind about him went far beyond that. "I'm attracted to you," he answered, at least half-honestly. "Usually, I prefer that the women I'm attracted to like me, at least a little."

"You've got your work cut out for you."

Michael laughed. "I've always liked a challenge. How about if we start by going out to dinner?"

Her face went blank. "Dinner?"

Michael chuckled softly. "You know, appetizer, salad and an entrée."

"Dinner," she repeated, as if getting used to the idea. "When?"

"Hmm, how about Friday? You're off that night, aren't you?" As if he didn't know. He probably knew Darcy's schedule better than she did.

"Yes, I think so." Her eyes had gone limpid, but suddenly a spark of suspicion flashed in them. "Just dinner?"

He nodded. "Just dinner. We'll reserve judgment on dessert."

"But I love dessert!"

"Me too, sweetheart. Me too."

DARCY HAD TO WORK hard not to gape when she opened her apartment door and spied Michael. Until the afternoon at the club, she would have sworn that Michael Davidson had emerged from his mother's womb dressed head to toe in Brooks Brothers attire.

And then, when she'd had the chance to get her fill of him almost in his birthday suit, she'd been completely shocked at the breadth of his shoulders, the ropes of muscles in his arms and legs. No doubt about it, Michael Davidson occasionally took off his suits and worked out. Hard.

And now, one more shock. He owned clothes other than power suits and bathing suits. He'd changed into navy pleated pants and a white cotton polo shirt. Overtop he wore a leather bomber jacket that looked like it had survived a stint in World War II. He had loafers on his feet and flowers in his hand.

No one had ever brought Darcy flowers before. Well, her father used to give her an orchid every Easter, but that was different. Michael Davidson was holding a full bouquet of bloodred roses. A lover's gift.

"Hi," he said, his lips lifting and his blue eyes crinkling handsomely. Darn. All the while that she'd dressed for her date with him, she'd managed to convince herself that he had ulterior motives. That he just wanted to soften her so that he could convince her to agree to his offer. She'd even planned the little speech she would give him when he showed up at the door.

"I'm sorry, Mr. Davidson, but agreeing to go to dinner

with you was a mistake. I admire the lengths you will go to for your stupid corporation, but I refuse to allow you to manipulate me through niceness. I see through your little plan, you turkey.''

Of course, she'd ignored the nagging voice in her head that kept wondering why, if she was so intent on refusing his dinner offer, she was still dressing in her favorite peach-and-green dress. She'd refused to analyze why she had washed her hair *again* and pulled it back from her face with barrettes. She'd refused to concede that the extra spritz of perfume was for anyone's nose but her own.

But staring up at his warm, sexy smile, every rational thought flew from her brain, and all that replaced it was the knowledge of how it felt to be kissed by him. To be touched by him. To be propositioned by him.

The man had actually told her he wanted her.

And Darcy was just crazy enough to want him, too.

She prayed she wouldn't do anything stupid tonight. But with her track record on dates, she didn't have an ice cube's chance in hell of getting through the night without embarrassing herself.

"You look great," he said after a long span of stupid silence on her part. She couldn't seem to make her tongue move. His presence in her doorway overwhelmed her. He was so big and tall, and she'd seen him nearly naked.

She knew that he had only a light sprinkling of crisp hair on his chest that tapered down to a single line that led directly to his navel…and beyond. She knew that even with his beautiful eyes closed, he was classically handsome and had the sexiest lips she'd ever seen. She knew that his chest was big and hard and she liked her breasts pressed to it. And she knew that she was suddenly eager to be intimate with a man. And, unfortunately, her body seemed to want it to be this man.

He held out the flowers. "These are for you."

Darcy took them, knowing that long after they died, she'd treasure them—her very first flowers ever. "Thank you," she said, burying her nose in one rose.

"You're welcome. May I come in?"

"Oh!" She stepped back. And caught her heel in the carpet. A flash of mortification burned through her as she realized she was about to fall on her rear end in front of him again.

Apparently Michael had been prepared, though. Because his hands shot out and steadied her. Grateful, embarrassed, electrified by his touch, she smiled tremulously. "Thank you."

"Close your eyes," he said, his fingers still searing her arms.

"Excuse me?"

"Close your eyes."

Darcy did.

"You're in the pool," he said in a soothing, gentle tone. "You're swimming, and you're in control."

Darcy didn't believe for a minute that she was in a pool. She was standing in her doorway having all kinds of kinky thoughts about a man whose hands could brand skin. But to please him she pictured herself in the pool, and amazingly, she felt a little calmer, a little more in control.

She opened her eyes and smiled. "It works!"

He flashed her one more bone-melting smile, before taking keys out of his leather jacket and gripping her elbow. Darcy knew that to get herself calmed down right now, she'd have to picture an entire swim meet.

MICHAEL DROVE Darcy from her Falls Church apartment to Old Town Alexandria. After parking his rented BMW near the dock, he took her aboard the cruise ship *Dandy*, which doubled as a restaurant as it plied its way up and down the Potomac. In his opinion, there was nothing more romantic than sharing wine and good food, all the while passing national treasure after national treasure.

Washington, D.C. at night was probably the most romantic city in the U.S. of A., in Michael's opinion. And he planned on wringing every ounce of romance out of this evening.

The notion baffled him. Darcy was far from his "type." But he had to admit that he liked a lot of things about her. Like her honesty. She had such expressive eyes, she'd never get away with lying to him. Which made her honest answers to his questions all the more appealing.

Her innocence made him nervous, but it excited him as well. For some reason, for once in his life he was happy that no man had been somewhere before him. He liked not having to wonder who else she'd been with, what other men had touched her body.

Innocence aside, he really liked the passion inside her. He had no doubt there was plenty to be tapped. And he wanted to heighten it to record levels.

Michael didn't know when his attitude toward Darcy had changed. He hated to think that it had everything to do with her looks and figure and nothing to do with her mind and personality. He was half-afraid her appeal was purely physical.

And if that was the case, he was going to end up hating himself. He'd only go and prove that he was just like his old man. And there wasn't a person on earth he despised more than his old man.

Shoving aside the unpleasant thought, he picked up the wine bottle and poured more sauvignon blanc in their goblets. Darcy smiled her thanks, and Michael returned it.

Her smile faded slightly as she stared at his lips. If he wasn't mistaken, that blaze in her eyes stemmed from hunger and desire. For him? Or for men in general? Had she finally reached a point in her life that any man would do?

The thought made his gut clench. Didn't she realize how special she was? Didn't she know she had a gift to offer up? Even though he'd avoided virgins his entire life, he sat in awe of her at the moment. He wanted to be the man to initiate her. Badly. Very, very badly.

As they passed under the Memorial Bridge, and by the splendor of the Lincoln Memorial on their left, Michael held up his glass in a toast. Darcy followed his lead.

"To friendship," he said, his voice sounding unusually husky to his own ears.

Her smile trembled just a little. "To friendship," she said, then started to touch goblets...with the force of a hammer. Michael pulled back just in time to avert disaster.

To a friendly affair, he thought as he sipped.

Darcy set down her goblet, licking her lips. She gazed out at the various monuments, all lit with spotlights and looking regal against the purplish night sky. Then she looked back at Michael, and something in her expression made his heart lurch. "What?"

"Tell me about your family."

His heart lurched again. He shrugged. "Not much to tell."

"Where are you from?"

"New York City, born and raised."

"Do your parents still live there?"

He was about to snap that his personal life was none of her damn business, but something stopped him. Her expression was so guileless, he knew she wasn't trying to unearth family secrets. He wondered how she'd react to the truth. And suddenly, he wanted to find out.

He took a sip of wine before answering her. "My mother still lives there. I have no idea where my father lives...or if he's still living at all."

That shocked her. Her goblet hit the table with a clang, sloshing some of the wine onto her hand. Michael gently pried her fingers loose from the stem and wiped her hand with his napkin, using it as an excuse to avoid her wide, questioning eyes.

"I'm sorry," she whispered. "Will you tell me what happened?"

Michael did look into her eyes then. There was no censure, not even pity. Just a certain sadness. For that he felt utterly grateful to her. "My mother's from a very prominent family. When she was eighteen, she and a friend went to the city on a shopping spree. They had lunch at Tavern on the Green. My mother fell fast and hard for the man who waited on them—"

"Your father."

"My father," he agreed, his jaw clenching. "They dated secretly for a few months, because my mother was well aware that her father would never approve. Unfortunately, my mother became pregnant—" he swallowed "—with me."

Darcy's jaw dropped like a lead weight. "Unfortunately? *Unfortunately?*"

Michael waved away the choice of words. "Anyway, her *boyfriend* wanted her to have an abortion, but she wouldn't hear of it."

"Thank God," Darcy murmured.

Michael liked that response. "So my mother and father worked up their courage and confessed to her father. Needless to say, he wasn't pleased. In fact, he was furious. Instead of letting them get married quickly and quietly, he actually tried to force my mother to get an illegal abortion. He kept her prisoner in the house. But somehow she managed to escape and run to my father.

"They got married, and a few months later, I was born. It was really rough for a while. My mother begged her father to give my father a job in his company, but he wanted nothing to do with her, with her husband or her child. He disowned her completely."

Darcy shook her head, her eyes bewildered. Knowing Ed Welham, he could understand her confusion. The idea of a father turning his back on his child would be inconceivable to her.

"A few years later, my sister Annie was born."

"You have a sister?"

Michael grinned at the thought of his daffy sibling. "Yeah. Anne Elizabeth. She's a couple of years older than you. She lives with us, too."

Darcy smiled, but then her smile faded. "What happened to your father?"

Michael's grin vanished, much as his father had. "One

day he just couldn't take it anymore, I guess. He went to the store for milk and never came home.''

"Oh, Michael! I'm so sorry."

"Don't be. We were better off without the son of a— Him."

"But...supporting two kids. All on her own?"

"Sometimes she worked two and three jobs at a time. Not only did she support us, she managed to send us to private school."

"She must be some woman."

"She is. She sacrificed so much for Annie and me."

Darcy's smile was wistful. "I'm sure she doesn't consider it a sacrifice, seeing how you turned out."

Darcy couldn't possibly know how much those words meant to him. His biggest fear in life was not returning big dividends on his mother's emotional investment. "Thank you," he said, his voice grainy.

She lowered her lashes. "So, what does your sister do?"

"She's an aspiring author."

Darcy looked up. "How wonderful! What does she write?"

"Romance and romantic suspense," Michael boasted. "She's really good, too."

Suddenly it occurred to Michael that he'd spilled his guts to this woman. He hadn't ever discussed his family background with an outsider before, and for the life of him, he didn't know why he'd done it now. Embarrassed, he searched for a way to change the subject.

"Do you remember your mother?" he asked, then silently debated biting off his tongue. His curiosity about Darcy had grown by leaps and bounds in the last few days, and he'd stupidly brought up a subject that had interested him. To his thinking, what Darcy Welham desperately needed was the guidance of a mother.

She looked at him, startled. After a pause, she swallowed and nodded.

"How old were you when she died, if you don't mind my asking?"

Darcy sipped her wine. "I was eleven."

"I'm sorry," he said softly.

Her eyes grew just a bit bright. "Yes, so am I." She set her glass down…on the edge of the table. Michael reached over and set it on firmer ground.

Darcy didn't notice. Her expression said she was years away from this moment. "It was wintertime. My parents were getting ready to open their fourth or fifth restaurant. This one in Chicago."

"The Chicago restaurant was their fifth," Michael said, without thinking.

"How—" Her mouth snapped shut. "Of course you'd know. You probably know more about the restaurants than I do."

Her look turned so glum, Michael covered her hand with his. "I'm sorry. Finish telling me about your mother."

"She was afraid of flying. So, instead of taking a plane she drove from Spokane to Chicago in a snowstorm. She made it all the way just fine. Then a block from the new restaurant site, she was broadsided by a semi."

Michael swore softly. No wonder Ed Welham had lost sentimental interest in his restaurants. But why hadn't Darcy?

He turned her hand over and made little circling motions in her palm with his thumb. "I think your mother would be very proud of you if she were still alive."

"You do?" Her free hand wobbled a little as she grabbed for her wine.

His hand shot out and picked the goblet up first. Then he passed it to her, holding it steady for a moment while he pretended to just want to use any excuse to touch his fingertips to hers. "Absolutely."

"Why?"

"Why not? You're beautiful, intelligent, sensitive, hard-working. And you're fighting to hold on to her dream. I admire that, I really do."

He really did, dammit. He really did. The only problem

was, her dream was interfering with his goal. And he never let anything interfere with his goals.

Unfortunately, he now had another goal. A conflicting goal. That goal was to make sweet, wild, all-night love to Darcy. He *had* to border on being certifiable.

"Thank you," she said in a soft voice. "That's nice of you to say. But I'm well aware of my...shortcomings."

Manners kept him from acknowledging that he was aware of several himself. "What shortcomings are those?"

She waved...nearly knocking over her wine. Michael silently pulled her goblet out of range. When her hand finally stilled, he pushed it back at her.

"You've been taking notes on my shortcomings for weeks. You know exactly what I'm talking about."

He squeezed her hand. "Darcy, grace is a state of mind. So is clumsiness. They're affected by your sense of self. As soon as you recognize that you are a valuable, worthwhile human being, I think those accidents will stop happening, at least with that much frequency."

She seemed uncomfortable with his analysis, and pulled her fingers from under his. The band started playing soft, classical music—Beethoven's "Moonlight Sonata" if he wasn't mistaken—and the waiter stopped and refreshed their water glasses.

Amazed at how relaxed he felt in Darcy's company, Michael drained his wineglass. Darcy refilled it and her own. And didn't spill a drop. Michael was so proud of her, he almost broke out in applause.

"Enough of family history," he said, admiring the smooth creaminess of her skin in the candlelight. She looked beautiful tonight, in a pretty flowing dress and her hair curling slightly around her face. "Let's talk about something pleasant."

"Something pleasant, huh?" she said. "Like what?"

Michael thought about it as he sipped on the wine. "Tell me the one thing you want to do most in the world."

"Have sex with you," Darcy blurted.

Michael's wineglass shattered as it hit the table.

6

"I'M SORRY!" Darcy said, for about the hundredth time in the last hour.

Passing a tourist bus on the parkway, Michael sighed. "Stop apologizing, Darcy. The wine wasn't your fault."

"I startled you."

He laughed. "That's an understatement."

"So it *was* my fault."

"You're welcome to startle me like that any time you'd like. Believe me, that kind of shock I can live with."

"I was forward," she said glumly. She sat pressed against the door of the Beemer, as if to get as far away from him as possible. They'd docked almost as soon as the waiter had finished clearing the glass and sopping up the wine. Darcy had been so unnerved, Michael had decided to take the scenic George Washington Memorial Parkway home. Not the shortest route to Falls Church, but, he hoped, the most soothing.

"I like that in a woman," he said, squeezing her hand.

Her head whipped around. "You do?"

"Very much. I like women who say what they feel, who tell me what they want." He glanced over at her and smiled. Her eyes had gone large as pies. "How else can I make them happy?"

"Women *tell* you what they want?"

"With any luck."

She digested that news for a moment. "Michael?"

He really liked the way she said his name. "Hmm?"

"I'm embarrassed to admit this, but I think you'd better know."

"What's that?"

"I...I've never had sex before."

He bit on his lip to stifle a smile. Her tone told him she was thoroughly disgusted with herself.

"I'm glad," he said, when he'd successfully squelched his grin.

"You are?" she squeaked.

"Sure." He took a breath. "I have an admission to make, myself."

"Don't tell me you've never had sex, because I won't believe it for a second."

"No, it's not that."

"And don't tell me you're gay, because I don't believe that, either. I don't care what everyone is say—" She gasped and slapped a hand over her mouth.

Michael did laugh then. "Don't worry, Darcy, I'm well aware of the rumor."

"You are?"

"Yes. And I want to thank you for staunchly defending my heterosexuality." He looked at her and grinned. "And, no, you're not Julia Roberts. You're much prettier."

She frowned. "Tom's got a big mouth."

"He just wanted me to know you weren't buying it."

"Why don't you deny it?"

"Because I don't think my sex life is anyone's business. And I really don't care what people think of me." He glanced at her. "Most people, that is."

Even in the dark of night, he could see her cheeks blush. "Okay, well if your secret isn't that, what is it?"

Michael swallowed. "The truth is, I've never been with a virgin before."

There was a long silence. Michael rolled his window down an inch, and the daffodil scent of Washington in springtime filled the interior of the car. An erotic image of him rubbing flower petals over Darcy's naked body, then breathing in the scent of her, filled his head. And other places. He shifted in the leather seat.

"Does it make a difference?" she asked in a soft, hesitant voice.

"I think it does." Michael took the Lee Highway exit. "Darcy, I think you've got this wonderful gift. The gift of purity—"

She snorted. "I don't consider that a gift. It's a curse, is what it is."

He waved. "Whatever you want to call it. I want you to make damn sure that you want to give that gift to me. I mean, your first time should be so special. And should be with someone you care about."

He held his breath. He was giving her the golden opportunity to back out, and he was at once scared to death, and hoping like hell, she'd jump on it.

"Are you asking me if I care about you?" she asked faintly.

His breath left him in a whoosh. "I guess so."

"I don't know. I don't know you well enough."

"That's probably the best reason to wait a while before you plunge into anything you might regret later."

"What about you? You could end up regretting it, too."

He pulled into Darcy's parking lot and stopped the car. Turning to her, he felt his lips quirk up. "Darcy, there's not a chance in hell I'd regret it. First of all, it's not going to hurt me, but it might hurt you a little. All that will happen to me is that I'll get great pleasure having sex with a beautiful woman. That'd be difficult to regret." He looked deep into her wide eyes and his smile disappeared. "I'd only regret it if you ended up regretting it. It's a major decision. One you need to take seriously."

His thumb pads caressed her wrists. "If all you're looking for is to experience sex, and any interested man will do, I want to be that man." He heaved a breath, because he didn't like that possibility. "If it's that you're sexually attracted to me, great." He heaved another breath, because he really liked that option. "But if you're looking for a long-term relationship, don't let me make love to you, because I'm not ready to promise that to you."

There, he'd said it. He'd laid it all out, and it was completely up to her. He knew he'd be sorely disappointed if she decided to give up on the idea, but he also knew he didn't want to take his pleasure now, and destroy her self-esteem later when he left her and returned to New York.

"I'd be an idiot not to be attracted to you," she said, staring at her lap.

Michael laughed softly. "I'll take that as a compliment."

"I mean, you're gorgeous."

"Thank you."

"And tall."

"Always have been."

"And you have a really great body."

Michael stifled more laughter. She sounded as if she were making a laundry list of why she should just go ahead and take the plunge with him. He could relate to that. "Thanks again."

"And...you're healthy, right?"

"Clean as a whistle."

"You're sure?"

"I give blood every time the Red Cross asks me. They haven't turned me down yet." He lifted her chin with his forefinger. "And I've never had unprotected sex in my life."

"I'm sorry for...asking."

"It's the nineties, sweetheart. You'd be a fool not to ask." He smiled. "If there's one thing I've learned about you, it's that you are no fool."

She took a noisy breath, but she met his eyes squarely. "I really want to go to bed with you, Michael. Does that make me foolish?"

He didn't know. But he *did* know what that declaration made *him*. It made him hot. It made him needy. It made him hard as marble. "I think you need more than one night to make certain what you want. I've pushed a lot of stuff on you this week, just because I tend to be an impatient man. Think about it for a couple of days, and then we'll talk."

He couldn't believe he was giving her yet another opportunity to change her mind. Where was the intelligent man who never passed up an opportunity when presented with one?

Shaking his head, he said, "Just promise me one thing."

"What?" she whispered.

"After you've thought about it, and if you decide you still want this, please let it be with me."

Her smile was shaky. "What if I fall head over heels in love with someone else tomorrow?"

The thought jabbed him more than it should have. He wanted to shout, "I won't let you!" Instead, he managed a smile. "Okay, okay. Let's just say that if you want to have sex, merely for pleasure's sake, you let me be the one to give you that pleasure."

She shook his hand. "Deal," she said, with a smile that lit up his heart.

"Come on, I'll walk you to your apartment." He climbed out of the car and came around to open her door.

"Michael?" she asked, as he helped her out of the car.

"Yes?"

"Would you come in for a little while?"

"If you want me to, sure." He looped an arm over her shoulder. "Why?"

"Because, I agree that I should probably think it over before I make the leap, but I'd still like to get in a practice session on kissing."

Michael nearly fell over. "Kissing?"

She looked up at him with a dreamy smile that he knew he could never resist. "Yes. I've really liked kissing you."

Kissing her. Damn. He didn't know which danger was greater. The danger to his body, or the danger to hers.

DARCY'S APARTMENT seemed smaller with Michael in it. He seemed to take up so much space, command so much awareness. He was larger than life in so many ways. And she wanted to make love with him more than anything in the world.

But she didn't want to appear easy, and she didn't want him to think she'd take the sex act lightly, so she knew she wasn't going to demand his company in her bed tonight. But, God, she was looking forward to it.

She prayed she wouldn't disappoint him.

She took his jacket from him and hung it in the hall closet, secretly brushing the collar over her nose to inhale the scent of leather and aftershave. God, even his smell was seductive.

"Do you want a drink?" she asked when she turned around.

He stretched his long legs out as he settled onto her sectional couch and draped his left arm along its back. Darcy knew which side of the couch she would sit on.

Michael smiled, making her insides turn all mushy. "Sure. What do you have?"

Darcy went to the hutch in the dining room and pulled out a bottle of cabernet. After popping the cork, something she prided herself on doing well these days, she brought two goblets back to the living room.

She handed him his wine, then set hers on the oak coffee table. "What kind of music do you like?"

"Do you have any Gloria Estefan?"

"Yes."

"That'd be great."

Darcy put Gloria Estefan's *Let It Loose* CD on the player. A loud crash sounded from above and she looked up, shaking her head.

"What the hell was that?" Michael asked, standing.

She wrinkled her nose. "The guys who live above me are notorious for their parties."

Returning to the couch, she picked up her wine. For some reason, she was feeling unusually competent tonight. Maybe it was the two glasses of wine she'd had so far. With that thought in mind, she took a large sip of the fiery burgundy liquid. It burned a path down to her belly.

Michael's lips twitched with humor.

"What?" Darcy asked, bemused.

"Are you fortifying your courage?"

"Do I have a reason to need courage?"

He took her glass and set it on the coffee table with his. Then pulled her into his arms. "I won't ever do anything you don't want me to. You're calling the shots, pretty lady. All of them."

She felt giddy with power. Testing his honesty, she said, "Kiss me."

"You want that, do you?" he murmured, his blue eyes going all smoky.

"Yes," she breathed.

While Gloria Estefan soulfully promised some unknown lover that she'd do "Anything For You," Darcy watched as Michael lowered his lips to hers.

At the first feather touch, her tummy lurched. At the second it dropped straight to her toes. At the third, she threw her arms around him and pressed herself to him, loving the steely hardness of his chest, his arms.

Something about that seemed to affect him. With a groan that sounded so very provocative, he gripped her lower back and deepened the kiss.

Darcy decided the man's lips were lethal weapons. They molded hers, shaping them to his, slowly, surely, coaxing them farther apart.

Darcy willingly let him direct the movement of her mouth as the world seemed to explode around her. Nothing existed but this man, his lips pressed to hers, his hands shaping her body to his.

She gasped when his tongue invaded her mouth. It was wonderful. Not disgusting at all. In fact, his tongue sweeping through her mouth excited her so much, she was afraid she'd do something dumb again.

Darcy tried to conjure the image of a pool. Mentally, she tried to dive in and swim. But the only swimming going on was in her head, where pleasure floated, and spiraled down through her, until she felt lost and weak. She had the feeling that if Michael let her go, she'd puddle to the ground. Her legs felt completely boneless.

He broke the kiss and stared down at her, a gleam in his eyes that Darcy thought might just be desire. "You're a—" he cleared his husky throat "—a quick study, Ms. Welham."

"Did I say you could stop?" she asked, amazed at her own brazenness, but desperately wanting to continue with the kissing.

"If you keep kissing me like that, I won't be able to stop. At anything."

She liked that idea. Cool, calm, note-taking Michael Davidson, out of control. "Kiss me again," she demanded.

He laughed softly. "Yes, ma'am."

And then he did.

Something funny was happening to parts of Darcy that weren't even connected to the lips he assaulted with such pleasure-giving thoroughness. Her breasts started aching, but not in a bad way. The heavy feeling in her stomach dropped to her thighs, where it stimulated parts of her that some might call shameful.

But she felt far from ashamed. In fact, she felt feminine and vulnerable, yet desirable and powerful. It was a strange, erotic combination. And so new to her, she had nothing to compare it to, no frame of reference.

From the way Michael's hands were roaming over her back, waist and hips, and by the way he groaned occasionally, and by the way this kiss was growing increasingly frantic, she knew she must be pleasing him, too. That thought made her heart soar. She wanted so badly to make him feel good, as he was making her feel.

Michael broke the kiss again and stared down at her. That was when she realized he was taking very deep breaths, and his eyes were so filled with passion, it made her heart leap with anticipation and fear.

"Am I doing everything right?"

He threw back his head and groaned. "Lady, I'm about to catch fire."

"Is that good?"

His laughter sounded a little desperate as he looked down at her again. "What you do to a man should be illegal."

That was good, wasn't it? She was almost positive it was. Especially when he was staring at her lips as if he wanted to devour them.

"Yes, that's good," he said, apparently seeing some doubt in her expression. "Want to feel how good?"

"Yes."

His hands slowly strayed down her back to cup her bottom. Darcy jumped a little but she didn't protest. Not when it felt so wonderful.

He pressed his hips to hers, giving her no doubt about how much he was enjoying their kissing.

"I want you," he said simply. "Feel how much I want you."

"I feel it," she whispered. "It feels great."

He laughed, low in his throat. "I'm very, very happy to hear it." He let go of her bottom and bracketed her face instead, brushing his thumbs over her cheeks. "Please ask me to stop, Darcy. I can't take much more without taking it to completion."

"Completion," she repeated. Yes, definitely, that's what that ache inside her was. She wasn't yet complete. And she knew enough about sex to know that to get there, she needed him inside of her. The thought made her already rapid pulse jump some more, and made the heaviness in her thighs and belly even heavier. Oh, yes, she wanted completion.

"I'd be lying if I said I wanted you to stop," she said.

His neck muscles corded. "Darcy, please…you have no idea how much it hurts a man to get so aroused and then not get to release all of that pressure."

The last thing she wanted to do was hurt him. She stepped back sharply. Unfortunately she forgot about the coffee table behind her. It hit her right behind the knee, and her leg buckled. She struggled to maintain her balance.

Michael, who was fast turning into her hero and tormentor both at once, grasped her arms before she could fall. He grinned. "I didn't want you to stop that fast."

God, she wanted to kiss him again. He tasted so yummy, and the sensations he created in her with just his lips were more than incredible. "Michael," she whispered. "Maybe we should…go to the bedroom."

His grin vanished. "Don't offer it to me, Darcy. I'm no philanthropist. I'll take it, take you."

"I'm pretty certain that's what I want you to do."

He gently moved her, then picked up their goblets and handed her one of them. Pointing toward her balcony, he said, "Let's get some fresh air, cool off, and talk about this a little more."

The last thing she wanted to do was talk. The very last thing. "Are you afraid to have sex with me?" she asked.

His head jerked back in surprise. "Afraid?"

"Afraid something bad will happen to you?"

He smiled, but still pulled her toward the door. "No, Darcy, I'm not afraid. I fully expect that if and when we make…have sex, it'll be one of the best things to ever happen to me."

"Then why are you refusing?" Her voice sounded a little sulky to her own ears. She hoped it didn't sound that way to him. "I don't understand."

Michael opened her sliding glass door. Immediately loud party sounds hit their ears. Music, voices, laughter all rang in the cool night air. He gestured Darcy out, then followed her and closed the door.

They moved to the iron railing, both leaning their forearms on it and gazing out at the midnight-blue sky. Stars winked overhead, and the air held a light floral scent.

Darcy decided to let him talk first. She felt a little hurt and confused that he wasn't taking what she so obviously wanted to give him. Especially since he had shown her just how much he wanted to.

It was long past time for her to learn about sex. And here she had a man all hot and bothered, and he still managed to resist. That wasn't exactly good for her ego.

"Darcy?"

She jumped. "Yes?"

"Why me?" he asked, without turning to her.

"I...don't know."

"I know that I started all of this. I know I kissed you first. And I know that I pushed you at the health club. But why, after twenty-five years, are you so willing to have sex with a man you don't even like?"

"I didn't say I don't like you."

He laughed. "You've made your feelings fairly clear the last few weeks. There's no love lost here. You and I have diametrically opposing goals."

"That's got nothing to do with this." She felt, rather than saw, him stiffen beside her. Her heart pinched, as her earlier suspicions came back to her. She straightened and turned to him. "Or does it?"

"I beg your pardon?" he said, straightening as well.

"Is that what all of this sudden attention is about?"

He hesitated, just long enough for Darcy to consider throwing her wine in his face.

He shrugged eloquently. "I'm not going to lie and say I'm not hoping to get you to listen to D.I.'s proposal, Darcy. Of course I want you to keep an open mind about that. But when I kissed you that first time, it was in response to *you* as a beautiful woman in distress, who I very much wanted to comfort and kiss.

"Today was the same way. I respond to you because I'm attracted to you. I would love nothing better than to pick you up and carry you to bed right now. That has nothing to do with you being a Welham and everything to do with you being a woman who turns me on."

Either he was an extremely accomplished liar, or he was utterly sincere. Darcy desperately wanted it to be the latter. And as he gazed unblinkingly into her eyes, she decided to believe him. Relief flooded through her, and she gave a shaky laugh. "I'm glad."

His teeth flashed like white beacons in the dark of the night. "Don't ever discount your appeal as a woman,

Darcy. I think you're sexy as hell. And your last name has nothing to do with that.''

"Kiss me," she demanded hoarsely. "Now."

He yanked her against him with a force that was thrilling. His mouth came down hard on hers, and Darcy, by now a seasoned veteran of two long and thorough French kisses, opened her lips to his immediately.

Their tongues mated. Darcy went weak all over again. By contrast, he seemed to go taut and gather strength. His hands moved over her body more insistently, bringing it to exquisite life.

Michael circled her waist with one arm, and cupped her head with his free hand. He tore his mouth from hers and started trailing hot kisses across her cheek, then down her throat. He bent her back as he sensitized her skin with his teeth and tongue.

She had a sense of hanging over some precipice, and vaguely realized she was hanging out over the railing. But his hold on her was so tight, she didn't feel any fear. All she felt was him, murmuring words she couldn't decipher against her throat.

As if through some distant horn, Darcy recognized the sound of a woman's squeal and then an exchange between two angry men. She ignored it all, threading her fingers through his thick, unruly hair.

She moaned as the sensations he created on her neck traveled with lightning-bolt speed through her body. She was lost. Completely lost. An ache bloomed between her legs. One she desperately wanted him to ease.

Three things suddenly penetrated her desire-fogged mind. One was a dull thud, coming from right above her. The second was Michael's body, jerking. He stumbled back toward the door, taking her with him. The third was the crash of glass against the brick outer wall of her apartment.

She looked up at Michael. His eyes were glazed, but not with passion. He grabbed on to her shoulders, more to steady himself than her, she suspected. Then his hands dropped, he wobbled once, and crumpled to the concrete floor.

7

A LAWN MOWER with a muffler problem was running rampant through Michael's skull. He kept his eyes squeezed tightly shut as he slowly regained consciousness, knowing that to let light in would be a serious mistake. He tried to acclimate himself through his other senses.

The antiseptic smell was unmistakable. He was in a hospital. Occasional droplets of water spattered on his right hand and forearm.

As his head slowly cleared, he suddenly realized that the racket sawing through his gray matter wasn't a lawn mower at all, but instead was the sound of someone loudly blowing a nose. As soon as the racket stopped, someone took his hand.

"Please, please, please," that someone whispered.

Darcy.

The events of that night came back in hammering spurts. The cruise ship, the drive to Darcy's, the kisses...the explosion at the back of his skull. Something had hit him in the head. Hard. And it felt, at the moment, that whatever it had been was still pounding behind his eyelids and at his temples.

Slowly, by degrees, he allowed his eyes to open. The light was a blinding spear straight through his brain.

"Michael?" Darcy whispered. "Are you awake?"

"Unfortunately," he croaked, closing his eyes again.

"Oh, thank God!" she said, squeezing his hand hard enough to break bone. "I'm sorry! I'm so sorry!"

"I'm sorry" seemed to be Darcy's mantra. If he remembered correctly, she hadn't had anything in her hands with which to bonk him on the head. Which meant that whatever had hit him had come from above. So what the hell was she apologizing for?

He cracked one eye open. "Darcy?"

"Yes, it's me. You're in Fairfax Hospital. They say you have a slight concussion, but you should be fine soon."

"How soon is soon?" Michael asked, wondering how long he'd have to live with the pulsing pain in his head.

"They want to keep you overnight for observation, but you should be able to go home tomorrow."

He looked at her. Her eyes were pink-tinged, her nose as red as Rudolph's, her golden lashes spiked with tears.

He'd never known any woman could look so beautiful when she looked so awful.

As gently as he could, he pried Darcy's hand off his. "What happened?"

"You were hit with a beer bottle."

"From the party."

"Y-yes," she said, her lower lip trembling. "And...and it's *all my fault!*"

She started wailing again, the sound jackhammering between his temples. But the pain in his head had nothing on the pain in his chest. Nothing on earth bothered him more than a woman's tears.

"Please don't cry," he pleaded. "It's not your fault, Darcy."

"Yes it is. It's always my fault."

"You're not the one who hit me."

"It might as well have been me," she whispered miserably. "If I could have got you into bed, then we wouldn't have needed fresh air and we wouldn't have been kissing on the balcony and you wouldn't have...wouldn't have been hurt."

With logic like that, Michael felt Darcy could probably start a whole new field of science. He considered asking her to raise the head of his bed, but thought better of it.

Gingerly, he turned his head toward the sound of her soft sobs. "Darcy, please don't cry!"

She made a pitiful attempt at stifling her sniffles. Leaning over him, she caressed his jaw, which, he had to admit, felt rather good. He covered her hand with his, just to keep it on his face.

"Thanks for taking care of me," he said softly.

Her hiccup sounded surprised. "You're welcome."

The squeak of rubber soles on flooring reverberated through his head like screeching tires. Darcy moved away, and a nurse who'd probably grown up with America's founding fathers took her place.

"Conscious, are we?"

Not giving him time to answer, she pried his eye wider open and shone a small light in it. His head screamed at the invasion, but he gritted his teeth to keep from crying out.

The old bat nodded and straightened. "Pupils responding nicely."

Michael refrained from responding not-so-nicely. "Can you raise the head of the bed a little?"

The nurse hit a button, and Michael's head slowly rose. Darcy came into his line of sight, wringing her hands at the foot of the bed. He smiled at her, and she tentatively smiled back.

"I want to go home," he told the nurse.

"Take it up with the doctor." She turned to Darcy, her hair shimmering a painful blue under the fluorescent light. "Five more minutes, young lady."

Then she squeaked out of the room.

"Come here, Darcy."

She came up beside him.

Michael took her hand. "Stop blaming yourself."

"I can't help it."

"Yes, you can."

She looked everywhere but into his eyes. "Did I ever tell you about my senior prom?"

Michael started to shake his head, only to wince. "No."

"Brad Fontaine asked me to go with him."

"Who was Brad Fontaine?"

"He was captain of the football team. Probably the most popular boy in school."

"He also had very good taste."

She shook her head. "He asked me on a dare. He had a bet with his buddies that he could survive a date with me."

Michael's heart constricted painfully. For some reason, he had the feeling this story was going to piss him off.

She finally met his gaze. Her eyes had dried, but there was a lifetime of hurt in them. She sighed softly. "The night was like a dream for me. I'd always had a secret crush on him, but always knew he was way out of my league.

"We were standing by the punch bowl, and all of his friends kept coming over and saying all of these strange things about bets and stuff. When Brad went to the rest room, Sara Jo Simms came over. Sara Jo was Brad's ex-girlfriend, and she'd been giving me nasty looks all night long. She told me all about the bet."

Dammit! How could kids be so cruel to one another? Michael thought of his own youth, and felt almost guilty for the ease with which he'd made it through school. Always having been one of the tallest, most athletic, and academically successful students, he'd never been the brunt of hurtful pranks.

"I was so embarrassed," Darcy continued. "Everyone knew but me. I should have known it was too good to be true. When Brad came back, I was shaking. He asked me to dance. All I wanted to do was go home." She forked her fingers through the hair at her forehead, pushing it back from her face. "Someone came up behind me and pinched my...bottom. I was so startled I dropped my punch." Her head shook sadly. "Brad slipped in the punch and broke his ankle. Because of that, he couldn't play football his freshman year in college. Not only that, but he lost fifty dollars, because he had to pay ten of his buddies five dollars each."

"Personally, I think the son of a bitch got what he deserved," Michael said. "So what's your point?"

"I went to see him in the hospital. He was so angry! He

told me that someone should lock me up and throw away the key, because I was nothing but a disaster waiting to happen.''

Michael called the jerk a few more choice names. Darcy met his eyes, and he flushed as a memory returned. *''Well, Darcy Wel-Wellington, you are a one-woman disaster zone.''* Her look told him she was remembering those words, too.

''Listen, Darcy—''

''No!'' She pulled her hand from his. ''Don't you see? He was right. You were both right. I wasn't meant to have a relationship, because if I do, I'll end up hurting someone.''

''That's not true!''

She stepped back. Michael wanted to reach out and grab her, pull her on top of him and kiss her senseless.

Darcy's chin came up, determination written in every rigid line of her jaw. ''Today was a mistake. I'm not going to let this go on, because I couldn't stand it if something even worse than this—'' she waved at his bed ''—happened to you because of me.''

''I'm willing to risk it.''

''I'm not.'' She stepped back again, nearly knocking over an IV pole. ''I'm taking care of the bill. Goodbye, Michael.''

''No!''

She gave him a tremulous smile, then turned abruptly.

''Darcy, wait!'' he cried, sitting up. Vertigo overwhelmed him, and he had to grip his head to try to ease the nauseating dizziness. When he finally got it under control, he looked up. Darcy was gone.

A devastating, not to mention surprising, sense of loss made him fall back on the pillow, holding his head.

''This isn't over, Darcy,'' he said to the empty room. ''Not by a long shot.''

8

DARCY FOUND the number she needed from the phone book and jabbed it into her cordless.

"Country Village Nursing Home," a woman answered on the first ring.

"Yes," Darcy said, glancing around her apartment and scowling. "I was wondering. Do you take donations?"

"Monetary donations?"

"Not exactly." She scowled again. "More like donations of plants, flowers, that kind of thing."

"Well, now, that's a rather…unusual question."

Darcy batted aside a palm as she paced her living room. "I have an… abundance of plants at the moment. I thought it would be nice if someone else enjoyed them."

"Well, isn't that thoughtful? If you bring them by, I'm sure our residents will enjoy them."

"Good. I'll get them there soon." She looked into her dining room. "I don't suppose anyone would want a few helium balloons?"

"Uh, no, I don't think so."

The doorbell rang. Again.

Sighing, Darcy hung up the phone and went to the door, looking through the peephole. Sure enough, another delivery boy. This one was dressed as a bellhop. She pulled a couple of one-dollar bills from her jeans pocket—money she'd learned to have at the ready at all times lately—and opened the door.

A goofy-looking young man with big ears grinned up at her. Darcy cocked her head. The kid had nothing but an envelope in his hand.

To her simultaneous astonishment and embarrassment, he dropped dramatically to one knee, whipped a card from the envelope, then placed a hand over his heart as he read the message.

"A message from Michael Davidson. 'Darcy—I lost you before I had a chance to win you. Please give me one more chance. Listen carefully to the words of this song. Please, Darcy, let it be.'"

Then, to her utter mortification, the kid started belting out a particularly bad rendition of the old Beatles tune.

Doors started popping open up and down the hall, as her neighbors tried to determine the source of the caterwauling. If there was any possible way Darcy could make herself disappear, she'd have done it there and then.

Somewhere to her right, a dog howled.

She'd never realized before just how very long the song was. Either that, or the kid was milking it, now that he had an audience. She hated to tell him, but she didn't think this audition would win him any additional jobs.

About a decade later, the boy finally wrapped up the song with a flourish, standing and bowing deeply. Darcy plastered a smile on her face and forced herself to clap, all the while plotting Michael Davidson's imminent demise.

She started to hand the boy his tip, but suddenly an arm—a suit-coat-covered arm—reached out from somewhere to the left of the door and handed the kid a twenty. The kid looked at the bill, eyes wide. His face split in a crooked grin, he snatched the bill, and disappeared.

Hands on hips, she waited for the rest of the body attached to that arm to appear. She didn't have to wait long.

He stepped in front of her, a determined scowl on his face that did nothing to detract from his breath-stealing good looks. She steeled herself. His scowl gave way to a smile as he looked her over.

She never should have admitted to him that she was affected by smiles. He'd taken to gracing her with his every time their eyes met these days. She had the feeling that it was his way of apologizing for calling her a coward last week.

But all of the gifts were for a different purpose altogether. He was trying to get her to change her mind about dating him. And she had to admit, he was doing a darn fine job of slowly chipping away at her defenses. That was, until he'd hired a young man with a voice that could peel paint to serenade her.

"Hi."

"Are you nuts?" she asked.

His smile faded slowly, and Darcy immediately regretted her harsh tone of voice.

He plowed both hands through his hair. "Probably."

She shook her head. "I'm sorry, I didn't mean to sound ungrateful, but—"

"What's it going to take, Darcy?" he asked, sounding a little desperate.

"I'm doing this for you!" she cried. Couldn't he see that? Didn't he realize that her fondest wish would be to have an affair with him? Didn't he know she was protecting him?

"Don't do me any favors," he said harshly.

"Stop sending me flowers."

"Stop being such a stubborn idiot," he shot back.

Well now, those weren't exactly wooing words. Darcy stepped back, grasped the door and slammed it in his handsome face.

ROMANCING HER *isn't working,* Michael scribbled glumly.

One damn frustrating female was Ms. Darcy Lynn Welham. Michael didn't think he'd ever had so much trouble trying to convince a woman to go out with him.

He knew she wanted to. He saw the need in her eyes whenever their gazes locked. He saw the regret whenever he approached her and she forced herself to back away from him. He saw the glum expression that crossed her face whenever one of the other girls flirted with him.

She was ruining his life for his own good.

Michael shook his head, feeling a vigorous urge to punch a few holes in the walls of Tom's office.

He glanced down at his list and scowled. So far, nothing had worked. And he'd run out of ideas. What the hell could he do to sway her? None of the normal channels were getting him anywhere. Short of kidnapping her and flying her to some remote island, he couldn't think of another tactic to try.

Slamming down the clipboard, he got to his feet and stalked out of Tom's office. Maybe if he strangled her, she might begin to listen to reason. Of course, she wouldn't be much fun dead. But at least she wouldn't be constantly in front of him, tormenting him, reminding him of something he wanted desperately but couldn't have.

Stomping through the kitchen, he didn't see Darcy. He nodded curtly to the employees who greeted him. He had the feeling his recent foul mood had them all a little puzzled, but frankly he didn't give a damn.

He found Darcy in the break room. Since there were two other waitresses in there with her, he didn't instantly confront her. Needing some excuse for loitering, he took his time pouring himself some coffee and mixing cream into it.

Wendy Walker, the little flirt, sidled up to him. He had the feeling she had decided to make it her personal mission to convert him to heterosexuality. And she didn't give up easily, something Michael could relate to at the moment.

"Howdy, cute thing," she said, batting her china-blue eyes at him.

"Hello."

"What are you doing this weekend?"

Quite possibly abducting a certain stubborn blonde, he thought. "I haven't decided," he answered politely. If he remembered correctly, Wendy Walker had asked him that same question every Friday since he'd been in D.C.

She laid a hand on his forearm, then rubbed it up and down his sleeve. He resisted the urge to throw it off.

"We're all going to George's Pub later. Want to come?"

Michael was about to refuse when he happened to glance over Wendy's auburn head and catch Darcy glaring at her. Specifically, glaring at the hand that massaged his arm in what Wendy apparently felt was a seductive manner.

Hmm, he thought, noting Darcy's narrowed look. He'd been so single-mindedly focused on pursuing Darcy, he hadn't considered winning her over by pushing her away. Or, more appropriately, by showing even cursory interest in someone else.

Well, nothing else had worked. He supposed he was desperate enough to put up with some overly flirtatious females who didn't do a thing for him. He shot Wendy the smile he'd until now reserved for Darcy alone. Since he heard a strangled hiss coming from the general direction of Darcy, he had the feeling she'd noticed.

"George's, huh?"

Wendy had probably been so prepared for another rejection, her mouth popped open a little as she gaped up at him. "Uh-huh," she answered, apparently rendered speechless.

"Sounds good. What time?"

It took her about six or seven seconds to locate her voice. "We all drop in as we get off work. Whoever gets off first goes over and holds a large table."

Michael fully planned to be the first to "get off." With Darcy.

"That's around ten," Wendy said.

He looked at Darcy. "Are you going?"

Darcy nodded mutely, her gaze still fixed on Wendy's hand.

Michael forced himself to return his attention to Wendy. He smiled again. "Okay, well, I think I'll stop at my hotel room and change clothes before heading over there. I'd hate to scare anyone off wearing a suit."

Her eyes gleamed. "Cool."

"See you then," he said, taking a sip of coffee before strolling out of the room, giving Darcy a wide, innocent smile as he passed her. She glared at him.

He could swear he heard her mutter, "Jerk."

Jealousy works, he thought, resisting the urge to laugh out loud.

JEALOUSY WAS WORKING all right. At the moment Michael was consumed with it. If the guy sitting beside Darcy at the large table at George's touched her one more time, Michael was going to deck the creep.

The man didn't work at Welham's. He was a stranger who'd had the nerve to take one look at Darcy and place her at the top of his acquisitions list. Darcy seemed a little unnerved by the attention. Michael was so busy keeping an eye on her, he hadn't had time to do any flirting of his own.

The son of a bitch leaned toward Darcy and whispered in her ear. Her eyes went wide and her hands fluttered. Michael had to choke back laughter when she bumped her mug of beer, dumping it directly into the overly eager jerk's lap.

Michael jumped up and headed to Darcy, before she took it into her head to try and dry the man's crotch.

"I'm sorry!" she cried, probably for about the twelfth time by now. She stared helplessly at the man, who was drying himself off with a cocktail napkin.

Michael held out his hand to Darcy. She stared up at him, hopeless, numbing horror on her face. He'd do just about anything to wipe the pain and embarrassment from her eyes.

The man who'd been trying to pick her up smiled tightly. "No problem."

Drawing Darcy to her feet, Michael grinned down at the guy. "That's Darcy's way of saying no."

"It was an accident!" Darcy protested.

Michael gave the guy a conspiratorial wink, before pulling Darcy from the table and out onto the dance floor. Amy Grant was singing something slow and sexy, and before Darcy could complain, Michael pulled her into his arms.

She tossed back her head and glared up at him. "Why did you make him think I did it on purpose?"

"Because I wanted to make damn sure he forgot whatever disgusting little suggestions he whispered in your ear."

"Why?"

"If anyone's going to make suggestions to you, it's going to be me."

He realized he sounded like a possessive, domineering, chauvinistic jerk, and he was way beyond caring. He'd had to sit and watch Darcy interacting with another man, and he hadn't liked it. Not one bit.

She stared up at him. "Forgive me for being so obtuse, Mr. Davidson, but last time I checked, that was my choice to make."

"So, I made it for you."

Her perfume wafted up to him, and Michael inhaled it deeply. He was far too happy to have Darcy in his arms again. Surprisingly, she danced rather fluidly.

"Next time I want you to make decisions for me, I'll let you know. I suggest you don't hold your breath while you wait."

God, she looked beautiful angry. "I was just trying to save you the trouble of letting the guy know you weren't interested."

"Who says I wasn't interested?"

Trying to tamp down his rising anger, he said, through gritted teeth, "He's not your type."

She gazed up at him in astonishment. God, she looked beautiful astonished. "How would you know what my type is?"

I'm your type, he wanted to say. But he didn't, too afraid she'd find several reasons to disabuse him of that notion. "I just do."

Her look told him how intelligent she considered that comeback. "Go ahead," she said, eyes glowing with humor. "Describe my type."

God, she looked beautiful when she was laughing at him. He grasped her waist and pressed her body to his. That felt really, really good. For her too, if the small sound she made in her throat was any indication. "You like a man who makes you feel...feminine."

Her eyes went wide and she swallowed. Michael started enjoying this verbal assault on her senses. He lowered his head...just a little. "You like a man who finds you sexy as hell, and shows you that in a million different little ways."

His hands started roaming her back. He sure did like the way she was built, all slender and curvy.

The Amy Grant song had long since ended, and Bruce Springsteen was now rasping out a pounding rock song. Still they slow-danced, oblivious to the writhing bodies around them.

Darcy shook her head, more to clear it than to indicate her denial, Michael thought. "I don't know if you're right or not."

"Why not?"

"I...I've never really thought about it."

"Think about it now." He brushed his lips over hers. "Do you like the way I kiss you?"

"Yes."

"Do you like the way I touch you?"

"Yes."

"Do you like the way I look at you?"

"When you're not mad at me, yes."

"Do you like *me,* Darcy?" he asked, his heart hammering. Her answer mattered to him. Too much.

"I'm almost certain I do."

He'd take that as a yes. "Are you attracted to me?"

"You know I am."

"Then I guess I'm your type, aren't I?"

"I guess you are."

"Not that turkey back at the table, but me."

"Can't women be attracted to more than one man at the same time?"

"No," he lied boldly, hoping she'd just take his word for it.

She digested that for a moment. "You're making that up."

"Women get reputations when they're attracted to more than one man at a time."

She clucked in disgust. "How dumb do you think I am, Davidson? I may not have much practice, but I grew up in the same generation you did. That kind of thinking went out with Donna Reed."

Michael had felt pretty certain he wouldn't get away with that, but he thought he'd give it a shot, anyway. He shrugged. "Okay, so sue me because I want you to be attracted to me exclusively."

She sighed. "I told you that wouldn't be wise. Who knows what will happen to—"

Just then Wendy Walker strolled up and interrupted them. "Come on, Darcy, don't hog him all to yourself!"

Thoroughly irritated by the interruption, Michael dropped his arms.

Darcy smiled at Wendy, a smile that didn't make it any higher than her teeth. "Oh, sure."

Wendy tried to turn him toward her. "Come on, you sexy thing, show me what you've got."

He turned back once to look at Darcy. She wasn't just frowning, she was actually glaring. She rose up and whispered in his ear, "You show her what you've got and I'll make sure to cut it off you."

His mouth dropped open. He stared at her as she marched off the dance floor. Yes, indeed, jealousy was working.

BY THE TIME Darcy returned from dancing with Michael, Luke, the guy she'd spilled beer on, had moved on to another of her co-workers. Darcy was relieved. She hadn't been comfortable with him, especially when he'd whispered in her ear that he'd like to take her home.

She wouldn't admit it in a million years, but she'd actually been grateful to Michael for rescuing her. For some reason, she felt comfortable with him. Well, not exactly comfortable, seeing as he made her nerves jump and her spine sizzle whenever he was near her. But still, he made her more relaxed, more at ease in her own skin. Why, she had no idea.

She sat down beside Anthony, who handed her a new beer. Smiling her thanks, she took a sip. Unconsciously, her eyes strayed back to the dance floor, seeking Michael's tall form.

She spotted him immediately. He stood out in a crowd like no man she'd ever met. It seemed as if a spotlight shone on him, highlighting him, making him the center of the universe.

Tonight he had on a pair of khaki pants and a snow-white oxford shirt, sleeves rolled to the elbows. He looked preppy and gorgeous and...like he was enjoying Wendy's company.

The two of them gyrated around the floor, both of them at ease with the rhythm of the song. Michael smiled down at Wendy, accepting her occasional hand on him without protest, it seemed.

Darcy saw green.

She didn't want him presenting other women with his high-voltage smile. She didn't want that errant lock of ebony hair gracing his forehead while another woman fawned over him. She didn't want his deep, growly voice and his sexy laughter directed at anyone but her.

She'd never felt this possessive streak before, had never known she was capable of jealousy. But apparently, she had it in her. Because as she watched Wendy wiggle her little body in front of him, Darcy wanted to rush over there and knock her away.

She took some comfort in the memory of his possessiveness earlier. At least her feelings weren't entirely one-sided.

"You've got it bad, Darcy."

Darcy dragged her gaze from the dance floor. "What?"

Anthony grinned. "I've never seen a pair of more lovesick eyes in my life."

"L-lovesick? Me?"

After a long swallow of beer, Anthony said, "I think it might be a lost cause, Darcy." He hugged her briefly. "I'm sorry, but I've heard rumors."

Darcy bit back a denial. After all, it wasn't her place to explain Michael's sexuality. Besides, she rather enjoyed the idea that the females at the table thought Michael was a lost cause.

All except Wendy, she thought waspishly, as she watched the woman try to engage Michael in a slow dance. Michael shook his head politely and clutched his throat as if he were dying of thirst. He swaggered back to the table, Wendy hot on his heels.

Darcy really liked the way he walked. He had a masculine grace and a long-limbed stride that made her stomach flutter. As did the deep blue gaze he bestowed on her.

His eyes narrowed slightly, and Darcy wondered why. She followed his gaze that had drifted slightly to her left. That was when she noticed that Anthony had draped an arm casually along the back of her chair. Darcy leaned forward to prove to Michael that Anthony was just using her chair as an armrest.

Michael sat down directly across from her, and Wendy quickly took the chair beside him, scooting it so close to Michael that Darcy couldn't have wedged a ruler between them.

Darcy drank deeply from her mug, trying to keep from tossing its contents onto the other woman. Wendy practically gushed as she looped her arm through Michael's and pressed her chest against him.

To his credit, he looked irritated. Not to his credit, he didn't disengage.

"You are such a good dancer," Wendy cooed.

"Thank you," Michael mumbled, then waved over the waiter. He ordered a round for everyone.

When the beers arrived, Michael drank half of his in one sip, then leaned toward Darcy, crossing his arms on the table in front of him. "What happened to Mr. Macho?" he murmured, for her ears alone.

It took Darcy a moment to remember who he meant. Especially since his eyes were gazing into hers, his lips were quirked in a half grin, and that damnable lock of hair had fallen forward again.

Not only that, but his skin had just a tiny bit of sheen to it, and it looked ruddy and tasty against the white of his shirt.

Her gaze dropped to his open collar. No hair peeked out near his throat, which Darcy should have expected, since she knew the exact spot on his chest where hair started growing.

As far as she was concerned, Michael Davidson was the only macho man in the bar. She forced her gaze back up to meet his. The amusement gleaming in his eyes told her she'd been looking him over a little too closely. Not only that, but she felt certain he'd asked her a question a long, long time ago, and she couldn't, for the life of her, remember what it had been.

"Excuse me. What?"

"I asked where the pickup artist went."

She opened her mouth, but a pouting Wendy interrupted her. "Mikey, honey, this is my *favorite* song in the whole wide world. You wouldn't refuse to dance with me to my favorite song, would you?"

A tic started in his jaw. "I don't dance with anyone who calls me Mikey, darlin'," he said, though he hadn't even turned to look at Wendy.

Wendy's pout doubled in size. "Michael, then."

"I'm sorry, Wendy, but I need to use the rest room," Michael said, untangling himself from the woman. "Maybe later," he added, smiling down at her as he stood.

Wendy hungrily followed his progress across the bar, before turning back to Darcy. "Tonight that man learns what it's like to be with a real woman."

Darcy kept a bland expression on her face, even as she pictured Wendy bald, once Darcy had finished pulling every artless auburn strand of hair from Wendy's head. "I thought you said he wasn't...inclined toward women."

Wendy studied her manicure. "I don't like to brag, but there isn't a man in this world I can't persuade to be inclined toward women, once I get him in bed."

Good thing for Wendy Darcy didn't carry weapons with her.

Wendy leaned forward and winked conspiratorially. "To tell you the truth, I don't really think he's gay, after all. I just think he needed to get out of his stuffy suits." She giggled. "I plan to get him out of a lot more, tonight."

That declaration made Darcy's blood run cold. In the couple of months she'd been in Washington, she'd watched Wendy conquer man after man, leaving every one of them panting for more. Darcy didn't know if she could handle knowing Michael was just one more of Wendy's conquests.

She knew Michael had probably gone to bed with many, many women in his life. That knowledge bothered her a little, but not much. She couldn't expect a man as attractive as he was to stay celibate. Besides, she'd been secretly glad that if and when they had sex, at least one of them would know what they were doing.

But if Michael ended up going to bed with Wendy, she knew she'd never sleep with him herself. She couldn't handle the thought of standing in some kind of sexual line for him.

In fact, she couldn't stand the thought that he'd been with *any* other women since he'd met her. That was asking a lot, she knew. There had been many, many nights in the last month that Michael didn't come into the restaurant at all. She couldn't imagine him just sitting alone and lonely in his hotel room. Not when he could come to a place like this and probably have his pick of women—women who'd have no qualms about climbing into bed at one crook of his long, elegant finger.

Darcy suddenly realized Wendy was still talking to her, and she hadn't heard a word she'd said. Not when her head was filled with images of Michael undressed, undressing the vivacious, man-eating woman in front of her.

Darcy shook her head. "What?"

"I said, I'm going to ask you to give me a ride home tonight. You refuse, okay? Make up some excuse, I don't care what. Then if he doesn't take the hint and offer me a ride, I'll just ask him outright."

Darcy wanted to help Wendy manipulate Michael about as much as she wanted to walk naked down Constitution Avenue. But to refuse would mean admitting she had an interest in Michael herself. And right now she couldn't bring herself to do that. She was too afraid Wendy would laugh uproariously.

At that moment Michael returned, and Darcy felt an ir-rational irritation at the rat for being so damn appealing to all of womankind.

Michael sat down, and Wendy immediately draped her-self all over him. The snake did nothing to stop her. Not one damn thing.

Darcy stood abruptly, bumping the table. Beer sloshed out of several nearby mugs, but thank God none of them spilled completely.

"Where are you going?" Michael asked.

Darcy dug through her purse to keep from having to face him. "Home," she muttered. Slapping a tip down on the rough wood table, she finally met his gaze. Big mistake. He was frowning. "I'm tired," she added.

"Oh, Darcy, do you think you could give me a ride home?" Wendy asked with saccharine sweetness.

Darcy wanted to scream, "Yes, you twit!" Instead, she sighed dramatically. "Do you think you could find some-one who lives closer to McLean? I'm really tired, Wendy." She matched Wendy's sweet smile watt for watt as she let her gaze slide to Michael. "Didn't you say you're staying at the Ritz Carlton at Tyson's Corner? Why, you and Wendy are practically neighbors!"

His eyes narrowed, causing sexy little lines to form close to his temples. He didn't say a word until Wendy turned to him in breathless anticipation. He smiled, but Darcy no-ticed the tightness in his jaw. She got a little thrill of plea-sure from the thought that he wasn't exactly happy playing chauffeur. "I'd be happy to take you home," he said, between closed teeth.

Darcy waved goodbye to the group in general, avoiding Michael's glare. She was happy that he wasn't happy, but that didn't mean much. Once Wendy got him alone, Darcy had little doubt she'd manage to change his attitude. After all, he was a man. Just a man.

As she whirled and made her way to the door, a thought just wouldn't stop pounding through her head.

He should have been *her* man.

9

DARCY WANDERED her apartment-turned-florist-shop, miserable. In the back of her mind she'd been praying that Michael would set land-speed records taking Wendy home, then race right over to her place.

She should have known better than to allow even a glimmer of hope to seep into her. She'd just set herself up to be disappointed.

Again.

Why had she allowed Wendy to manipulate her into handing Michael over on a silver platter? Why didn't she have the backbone to fight for him? The answer was simple, really. Because she knew if she were Michael, she'd rather be with petite, adorable, flirtatious Wendy than tall, gangly, klutzy Darcy.

Darcy inhaled the scent of the fading roses, then checked her watch. It had been two and a half hours since she'd left George's Pub. She squeezed her eyes shut, trying to drown out images of Wendy in Michael's arms, his chiseled lips roaming over her skin, his fingers exploring her feminine charms.

With a groan of disgust, Darcy stomped into her bedroom and threw off her clothes. Michael wasn't coming. She might as well try to get some sleep. Darcy changed into her favorite sleep attire—a huge, comfortable, flannel Seattle Seahawks nightshirt.

In the middle of brushing her teeth, she thought she heard a knock on her door. She stopped for a moment and turned off the water. Nothing. Shaking her head, she continued to rinse out her mouth. Pipe dreams.

The sound came again. This time Darcy was certain of it. She couldn't think of a single person who would knock on her door at two o'clock in the morning.

Except...

Darcy grabbed a hand towel and wiped her mouth as she raced out of the bathroom, down the hall to her door. She took a quick peek through the peephole, but no one was there. Disappointment raced through her, and her head hung low. She must have imagined it after all.

Then she suddenly felt and heard the sound of heavy footsteps approach. They stopped in front of her door and Darcy froze, half in fear, half in anticipation.

"To hell with it," she heard a voice mutter. An unmistakable voice. "I'm waking her up if I have to blow the building down to do it."

The big bad wolf outside her door was Michael.

Without thinking, she yanked the door open. And nearly got punched in the nose by Michael's fist. He grabbed his hand back just in time.

They stared at each other for an eternity. Then Michael's eyes made a long, slow sweep over her body. That's when Darcy realized she'd pulled open the door while nearly half-naked.

Well, actually she was exposing less skin than she had in her bathing suit. The nightshirt fell to midthigh, and covered her arms to her wrists.

Still, when she saw his eyes catch blue fire, Darcy started taking unconscious, shallow breaths.

She was acutely aware, suddenly, that she had nothing on under the nightshirt except a pair of skimpy panties. Her breasts—her unbound breasts—tightened almost painfully.

Michael visibly swallowed. "May I—" he coughed "—come in?"

Darcy backed up a step, mute with burgeoning joy. He'd come after all!

He didn't immediately follow her inside. In fact, his gaze dropped to her bare legs and he swallowed again, twice.

Darcy was torn between the desire to inch her nightshirt

up higher to give him a better view, or to run into her bedroom and wrap her ankle-length terry robe around her.

In point of fact, she did neither. She just stood still as a statue and watched him fight some emotion she couldn't identify.

Finally he took a step into her apartment. And pulled a bunch of daffodils from behind his back.

Darcy took them automatically, burying her nose in them. The man had a flower fetish. She liked that about him.

"I picked them out front. Hope nobody minds."

That news jolted Darcy out of her Michael-induced lethargy. "You picked Mrs. Wisonhurst's daffodils?"

"Uh-oh. Big mistake, huh?"

Darcy laughed softly. "Only if she caught you. And I doubt even Mrs. Wisonhurst would be snooping out her front window at two o'clock in the morning."

She headed for the kitchen to look for something to put the daffodils in.

"I'm sorry I stopped over so late," Michael said from behind her.

"I wasn't sleeping," she returned, glancing over her shoulder. Michael's eyes were glued to the back of her legs, so he didn't stop when she did. He bumped right into her.

Darcy lurched forward, but Michael's arms came around her to stop her fall. Only problem was, his hand landed directly on Darcy's left breast. They both froze.

His palm was a searing brand even through the flannel. Darcy was embarrassed to feel her breast respond to his touch. It seemed to swell and tighten at once. He couldn't help but notice.

After what seemed like an eternity, but was over far too soon, he removed his hand from her breast, managing to brush his fingertips over her beaded nipple while his hand moved to her shoulder.

Mortified at the rush of heat and moisture that pooled between her legs, Darcy stood stiff, her back to him.

"Darcy," he whispered, turning her inexorably around to face the music. To face him.

Knowing her cheeks were flaming, she kept her head down, hoping her loose hair would hide the raging blush.

"Darcy, look at me."

He grasped her chin and raised her head. But he couldn't control her eyes, which she kept trained on his chest.

"Please, look at me."

Her gaze crept up his chest to his jaw and stopped at his nose.

"I'm sorry. I didn't do that on purpose. I'm not the kind of guy to try and cop a cheap feel."

Her eyes snapped up to his. Was he calling her cheap? No, not with that half worried, half passionate blaze in his eyes. "I know," she squeaked finally.

He hissed a swearword, tore the flowers from her hand and threw them on the kitchen floor, then crushed her against him. His mouth covered hers feverishly and his hands left her shoulders to plow through her hair.

Darcy's knees turned to jelly, and her heart leapt into a gallop. She put her arms around his waist, relishing the pleasure gushing through her.

Michael's tongue invaded her mouth, and she met it thrust for thrust. Just like the last time, her response made him growl in his throat. She loved it.

Darcy allowed her hands to roam over his waist and back. She even let them slip down to wander over his trim hips. Then she returned to his back, loving the way his muscles responded to her touch.

Michael broke the kiss, trailing his lips across her cheek to her ear. Darcy gasped as his tongue traced its shell, then he moved to nibble her lobe gently.

She'd been so caught up in the tactile sensations he evoked, her other senses had taken temporary leave. But as his jaw brushed over her chin, suddenly her sense of smell returned.

Perfume. The man smelled like cheap perfume. Wendy Walker's cheap perfume.

Darcy reacted instinctively. She pushed at his chest and he let her go. Before she could think things through, her palm cracked against his jaw.

Dazed and confused and still consumed with lust, Michael took a step back, his hand lifting to his burning face.

Darcy's eyes blazed with anger. Why, he had no idea. Was it a delayed reaction to his accidentally grabbing her breast? "What the hell? I told you I was sorry!"

She started jabbing a finger in his chest, and Michael continued to stumble backward toward the living room as she stalked him.

"You no-good snake!"

"Darcy—"

"How dare you come over here after being with her?"

"Darcy—"

"What were you trying to do, see how many women you could conquer in one night?"

"No. Listen, Darcy—"

"No, *you* listen. If you think I'm just going to fall blithely into bed with you, hours, maybe minutes, after you've been with another woman, you are sadly ill-informed."

"But I haven't—"

"Now get out of my home and don't ever come back!"

Michael backed into a potted palm, and its fronds engulfed him. He batted his way out, then grabbed her rigid shoulders. "Listen to me!" he growled, giving her a tiny shake to get her attention. "I was never with her! I took her home, that was all."

"I hate to tell you, Davidson, but perfume transfers from body to body by osmosis."

Michael nearly groaned. But he didn't get the chance. Because, if possible, Darcy went even stiffer and her eyes widened dramatically before narrowing into green slits, like the eyes of a cat about to pounce. Only Darcy could look beautiful outraged.

"You jerk," she whispered.

"What now?"

"Have you taken to wearing lipstick as well as cheap perfume?"

Uh-oh. Maybe he should have run home and showered before dropping in on Darcy. Problem was, he'd been so desperate to see her, he hadn't thought of his appearance. And he thought he'd scrubbed his lips hard enough in the car to get rid of any traces of the disgusting stuff. "I have lipstick on me somewhere?"

"On your collar."

Well, that wasn't so bad. He could explain that.

She crossed her arms and looked at him disgustedly. "And now that I think about it, faint traces of the taste of it on your lips."

But probably not that.

"Calm down a moment and listen to me."

"Get out."

"Darcy, give me a chance to explain," he said, trying to keep his voice calm, even. He didn't want the panic rising through him to show, because he was afraid she'd misinterpret it as guilt.

"What's to explain?"

"Nothing happened between Wendy and me."

"Right."

"There's a perfectly reasonable explanation, if you'll reasonable enough to listen to it."

"Reasonable!" she squealed. "Are you calling me unreasonable?"

Women! Damn, would he ever understand how their minds worked? He sighed. "No, I'm not calling you unreasonable. I'm asking you to give me a chance to explain."

Her body relaxed an infinitesimal amount, but Michael considered that a major victory. "Let's make drinks—I could use one right now—and sit down. Give me five minutes of your undivided attention. I promise, I can explain."

"But will it be the truth?"

"One hundred percent."

Her crossed arms dropped to her sides. Another major victory.

"One drink. Five minutes," she said.

As A RULE, Darcy confined her alcohol consumption to wine with dinner and a beer or two when she unwound with her co-workers after a shift. Although she had a fully stocked liquor cabinet, she rarely touched hard liquor.

Tonight, she chose to have a martini.

Michael opted for a vodka and tonic.

After several abortive attempts at mixing their drinks, she let Michael take over. He mixed and stirred with an efficiency and grace she both admired and envied.

What was wrong with her? Why couldn't she perform even the simplest tasks? What gene had bypassed her?

She watched his fingers pluck ice from her freezer, his hands pour the alcohol, his wrists stir the drinks, his arm calmly hand her the martini, and she blinked back tears.

It was all so simple. So very simple. And Darcy Lynn Velham couldn't accomplish even that.

"What's wrong, Darcy?" Michael asked softly. He sipped his drink. "If you really want me to leave, I will."

"No, it's not that. I'm—" she swallowed "—engaging in a bout of self-pity. I'm sorry."

Michael's eyebrows shot up. "Self-pity? Why?"

Darcy bit down on her lower lip, then shook her head. "Never mind."

Michael took her elbow and tugged her into the living room. He tucked her into the corner of the sectional couch, then sat down beside her, not all that close, but close enough that the energy radiating from his body still touched her. Warmed her. Excited her.

"Give," Michael said, gently but firmly.

"It's stupid."

"I'll be the judge of that." He draped his arm along the back of the couch.

He was so attractive. He was so sexy. He was so darn masculine, Darcy wanted to jump his bones. But his eyes compelled her to talk instead. "I've always wanted a dog," she said, her voice low and slightly shaky.

Michael nodded, as if that were the most normal conversation starter in the world. "Why haven't you gotten one?"

Darcy worried her lower lip. "When I was four, I asked for a dog for my birthday. My dad sat me down and described the responsibilities involved in owning a pet. He offered me a compromise. He said I could get some fish, and if I took good care of them, he'd get me a dog." She blinked, trying not to let it hurt.

"I'm not going to like how this story ends, am I? This is another senior-prom thing, isn't it?"

"I killed them."

He swore. "Darcy, fish aren't known for their long life spans."

"I'd owned them for three days."

He swore again. "Maybe they were already sick."

She really liked the way he tried to defend her, but she wouldn't allow him to let her off the hook. Shaking her head, she said, "I fed them in the morning. That third morning, they seemed so hungry, so I added an extra pinch of fish food. They really liked that, and I wanted so much for them to like me. So about an hour later, I fed them a little more. They ate it up. So—"

"I get the picture," he interjected. "Darcy, I think statistics prove that one out of every two kids who owns fish feeds them to death. It's a rite of passage or something."

"You're making that up."

"No, really. In fact, I think it's almost a rule."

He looked so sincere, Darcy had to laugh. "That's sweet, really, but the fact of the matter is, I couldn't even handle fish. My dad felt so bad for me, he offered to get me a dog anyway. But I was afraid of killing it, so I said no."

"Damn," Michael muttered. How could any one woman have survived so many hard-luck stories? And why did her stories bother him so much?

Because he cared about her, that's why.

Okay, so he finally admitted it. He cared about Darcy Lynn Welham, the klutz, the calculator brain, the lover of dogs. No matter that she was a threat to his physical and emotional well-being, he cared. And he wasn't going to stand by and let a lifetime of hurts get her down. What was that saying? Something about today being the first day of the rest of your life? Today, tonight, this morning, whatever the hell time it was, was the new beginning for Darcy.

"You know, I think it's time you get a dog."

She choked on her drink. "I'd kill it."

"You'd love it. You're a grown, mature woman, and it's about damn time you stop this stupid cycle."

Her look told him she took exception to his tone. "What cycle?"

"This stupid, damn, self-perpetuating cycle that feeds the myth you're some incompetent, bumbling child who can't accomplish one task well." He slugged down half his drink, angry at her parents for not taking this step a long time ago, angry at Darcy for having so little self-esteem that she considered herself unworthy, angry at himself for even thinking about how much he wanted to take her to bed while he had so much more foundational work to do first.

He slammed his glass down on her table. "Close your eyes."

"Am I going swimming again?"

"Diving. Close your eyes."

"This is si—"

"Close your eyes, dammit!"

Darcy's eyes slammed shut.

"Now, what's your favorite dive?"

"Jackknife."

"That's not aspiring too high," he said skeptically. "Maybe something a little more difficult?"

She popped one eye open. "That's why I like it. It's simple, clean, and feels right. Nope, I'm sticking with the jackknife." Her eye shut.

Seeing as he was devouring her features, her darling nose and stubborn chin and long, golden lashes and lovely cheekbones, it took him a moment to remember what they were doing. Hell, right now he wasn't certain where they were. His concentration was focused completely on Darcy.

Darcy, right.

Unable to resist, he dropped a quick kiss on that darling nose, then said, "Set up for the dive."

Her lips curved up. After a moment, she said, "Ready."

"Let her rip, sweetheart."

He closed his eyes, too, and remembered the perfect jackknife she'd executed that day at the health club. He pictured it in slow, slow motion, giving him time to savor the grace of her movements, the clean lines of her body, the almost nonexistent splash as she sliced into the water.

He felt his lips lift in an appreciative smile. When he finally opened his eyes, she was already looking at him, a puzzled smile on her own face. Apparently she'd pictured it in real time.

"Beautiful," he whispered, meaning every syllable. "That dive was beautiful."

"Thank you," she whispered back.

"Take the square root of one-forty-four, multiply it by fifty-five squared, divide that by nine and add four thousand, two hundred and thirteen. What have you got?"

"Eight thousand, two hundred, forty-six point three, three, three into infinity," she said without hesitation.

Michael shook his head. "If I had my calculator, I'd be able to check your answer."

"It's right," she said, her chin coming up a notch.

That's it, sweetheart. "If you say so," he said, hoping he looked skeptical.

"You don't believe me?" Her eyes flamed with indignation and challenge.

"Of course I do," he said, patting her hand.

She slammed her own glass down—without breaking it, thank God—and marched into the kitchen, missing Michael's triumphant grin.

Coming back with a hand calculator, she mumbled the equation he'd given her and jabbed the buttons at the same time. Without looking up, she'd sidestepped one of the many plants he'd given her, walked around the coffee table, sat down and crossed her long legs.

Michael's spit turned to dust. There was so much grace trapped in that body, begging to be set free. So much grace, being held hostage by low self-esteem and a past filled with overwhelming, unforgettable hurt.

She thrust the calculator under his nose. "See?"

"You could have punched anything in there."

Her mouth dropped open. "Are you accusing me of cheating?" Her tone was incredulous. She punched the clear button and started over.

Michael laid a hand over hers to stop her. When she looked up, he smiled. "I knew it was right. I've seen you in action. I know you've got some kind of incredible gift with numbers."

"Then why—"

"I was teasing you, sweetheart."

"Oh."

He grabbed his drink, took a sip, then started rubbing the condensation with the pad of his thumb. "You know, when you were doing something you felt confident about, you didn't once think about being clumsy or inadequate. You were in your element. And babe, you are something magnificent to behold when you are in your element."

She blushed all the way up to the roots of her hair. Her suddenly shaky hand dropped the calculator, then reached for her drink, knocking it over. "Oh, damn!"

Michael set down his own drink and took her trembling hands. "Leave it."

"But I need to—"

"Kiss me."

She forgot to be nervous. Her chin tipped up. "I'm not touching your lips. I happen to know where they've been tonight."

"But—"

"And you still smell like a perfume factory."

"But—"

"And I don't think Wendy would approve of you being here."

Michael slapped his hand over her mouth. "Lucky you. Now you get to hear my side of the story." He pulled her stiff body against him. "We might as well be comfortable."

"Mmmmmpht."

"My thoughts exactly." He grinned down at her. "Now, here's the deal. I took Wendy home. She insisted that I walk her to her apartment in case her ogre of an ex-boyfriend was waiting for her."

"Mpphhhht?"

He cautiously lifted his hand away. "What?"

"I said, and you bought that?"

"Well, no, not really. Unfortunately, my mother taught me it's not polite to question a lady's veracity."

Darcy snorted, but she stayed silent, watching him warily.

"Anyway, when we got inside her apartment she—" he tugged at his collar "—sort of...well—"

"Attacked you?"

"Exactly!"

"Right."

"It's the truth!" he said, stung.

"Let me guess. You resisted her, right?"

"Right."

"Right."

"It's the truth!" he said again.

"How did you get lipstick on your lips?"

"She staged a full-frontal attack, Darcy."

"Poor baby."

"If you remember correctly, I didn't ask to take her home."

Darcy had the grace to look slightly ashamed. "I...I didn't think you'd mind."

"You thought wrong. I minded a great deal."

She searched his face. "No one's ever turned Wendy down before."

"What do you know? I'm a first."

"You...didn't kiss her?"

He shook his head. Holding up three fingers, he said, "Scout's honor. She caught me when I wasn't looking. I broke the kiss as fast as I possibly could."

"Did you...enjoy it?"

"I would have enjoyed it a lot more if I was attracted to her."

"Everyone's attracted to Wendy."

"Wrong again." He picked up a lock of Darcy's hair. "My tastes are running to blondes these days."

Color bloomed on her cheeks. "Flirt."

"Is it working?"

"Maybe."

He tugged her closer to him, and Darcy wiggled, settling into the circle of his arms. "Thank God something finally has."

"What?"

"Nothing," he said quickly. Then, before she could probe further, he kissed her.

The taste of her made his blood thrum through his veins. Her lips felt so right under his, so soft and pliant. Michael thought he could spend the next decade kissing her. The idea appealed to him on every level. Especially the base, male level that came roaring to life when Darcy was near him.

Every nerve he possessed cried out for him to toss her down and tear the flannel nightshirt from her body, to stroke her and kiss her and lick her into awareness and beyond.

Breaking the kiss, he took a deep breath. He ran his tongue along the shell of her ear, as his fingers skimmed up her hips, to her waist. He hesitated there for a fraction of a moment, then gave in to his overwhelming desire to touch her breast.

She made a soft, gaspy sound, but she didn't protest. Her fingers dug into his chest. Her breast felt full and lush and he was going to die if he didn't get to suckle on it soon.

"I want you, Darcy. Right here. Right now," he growled into her ear.

"I think," she whispered, "I'd like my first time to be on a traditional piece of furniture."

He raised his head and stared down at her. "Are you saying what I think you're saying?"

Her lips were parted and moist, her breaths ragged. "Yes," she said, her eyes half-hooded.

"You want me, too?"

"On one condition."

"What's that?" he asked, then held his breath, praying it wasn't an impossible condition.

"Do you have protection?"

Michael jumped to his feet and fumbled with his wallet. "Thank God," he mumbled when he spotted the two foil packets. If he had his way, he'd have a couple of cases of condoms delivered. But he'd start with two. He looked up. "Yes."

She rose and smiled at him—a serene smile that made his bones quiver. He had the feeling she had no idea what she was in for. And suddenly he was as nervous and scared as a horny kid.

He wanted it to be good for her. Scratch that. He wanted it to be fantastic for her. "You're sure?" he asked her, again, for the last time.

"Yes," she said, making him one happy guy. One nervous, happy guy.

"Where's your bedroom?"

10

MICHAEL GLANCED around Darcy's bedroom and grinned. Her comforter was peach and lime-green and sky-blue and pretty, with a frilly skirt gracing the bottom. Her furniture was blond oak. She had candles everywhere, all shapes and sizes, all colors and scents.

Her room looked and smelled like heaven. Like Darcy.

He turned back to her. She stood studying her painted toenails, her fingers alternately clutching and releasing the hem of her nightshirt. Every so often she swallowed. Hard.

"I like your room."

She looked up. "You do?"

Nodding, he said, "It's pretty and feminine, just like its owner."

She didn't answer him. Michael pulled her into his arms. That's when he realized she was trembling.

He brushed her hair back over her shoulder and lifted her chin. "Darcy," he whispered, "If you're having second thoughts, tell me. I don't want to rush this if you're not ready."

"It's not that."

"Then what is it?"

"I feel so stupid," she blurted. "I'm twenty-five years old and I have no idea what to do. I mean, I know the logistics, I know what's supposed to go where, but I don't have—"

"Shhh." He dropped a kiss on her lips. "This first time, you just relax and let me do it all."

"But that seems so selfish."

"Of me, it probably is." He smiled gently as she

searched his eyes. "You have no idea how much I want to do it all with you. How many times I've fantasized about this."

"A man's never seen me naked before."

"I can't tell you how happy that makes me."

"What if you don't like how I look?"

His hands stroked her back soothingly. "I sincerely doubt we'll run into that problem."

"I'd die."

Michael glanced around the room. That's when he realized that although Darcy had dozens of candles, not one looked like it had ever been lit. Probably smart on her part. "Do you collect candles?"

She nodded.

"Is there some rule against lighting them?"

She shook her head. "I just didn't...want to take any chances."

Definitely smart on her part. "Do you mind if I light some?"

"No."

"Where are your matches?"

"There's a lighter in the table by the bed."

Keeping his arm around her waist, he turned and opened the table drawer and pulled out a disposable lighter, pocketing it. Then he leaned over to close the door and flick off the light, blanketing them in soothing darkness.

He cradled the back of Darcy's head, then lowered his mouth to hers. In the darkness, he missed the first time, kissing her jaw. But he worked his way up until their lips were moving together in an ageless, seductive rhythm.

He lifted his head. He could barely make out her features—only the light from the half-moon filtering through her gauzy window curtain. "I'm going to undress you, Darcy."

"You are?"

"Yes. In the dark. Then I'm going to lay you down on the bed and light a few candles. You can tell me to stop any time you like, when you start feeling uncomfortable with the illumination. Fair?''

''Fair.''

Michael had already figured out that it wouldn't take much to get Darcy naked. By his count, she was only wearing two pieces of clothing. He took a deep breath, then slipped her nightshirt over her head. The scent of her skin reached him, filling him instantly with longing.

He forced himself not to toss her on the bed and cover her body with his. He forced himself not to even touch all of those parts of her he was dying to touch.

Kissing her, he eased her bikini panties over her hips. They dropped from his fingers, and Michael felt her step out of them. He kissed her again, cupping her face, trying to keep his mind from imagining what kind of goddess stood in front of him, naked and prepared to let him touch her.

He led her to the bed and laid her down. He could barely make out her silhouette, but it was enough to answer one question. ''You've got nothing to worry about. Your body's beautiful.''

''How can you tell?''

''I've got great night vision.''

''Oh!'' She scrambled under the covers.

Michael stifled a smile. By the time he was finished with her, she'd be so proud of the effect the sight of her body had on him, she'd be dancing naked around the bedroom.

He hoped.

He reached for a candle on her nightstand. ''Darcy, there are a couple of basic rules to lovemaking. Have you heard them?''

''No.''

''May I tell them to you?''

''Please.''

''Okay. Number one, the man and woman have to be perfectly honest with each other. Without honesty, the experience won't be as wonderful as it could be.''

''Honest about what?''

He lit a second candle, carefully not looking at her. "Honest about what feels good and what doesn't."

"Oh."

He lit a third candle. The scent of vanilla floated up to him. After setting down the candle on her dresser, he moved to her vanity. "When I touch you, I want you to tell me where it feels good, and how it feels."

"Okay."

"I'm going to kiss you, Darcy. And not just your mouth. I want you to tell me where you like me kissing you."

Out of the corner of his eye, he saw Darcy squirm a little under the sheet. He lit two more candles, then turned back to her. The candlelight bathed the room golden. Darcy's hair was spread out on the pillow, and her green eyes glowed.

"I'm sure you know that the first time for a woman is sometimes a little painful."

"Yes."

"Well, I don't pretend to have experience in easing that pain, but I'm going to give it my best shot, all right?"

"Yes."

"Just promise me you'll relax and tell me exactly what you like and don't like."

"Okay."

"Is that enough light?"

"Yes."

Michael dropped the lighter back into the drawer, then pulled out his wallet and laid the two condom packages beside her alarm clock.

He kicked off his shoes while he unbuttoned his shirt. "Inch the sheet down your body, Darcy. I want to see you."

She hesitated.

"I've touched you. I know the shape of you. Believe me, I approve. Let me see you, Darcy." He shrugged out of his shirt. "There. Here's my chest. Let me see yours."

She inched the sheet down to her waist. Michael sucked in his breath. "My God!"

The sheet zoomed back up to her chin.

"Don't! God, Darcy, you're beautiful."

While he unbuckled his belt, he watched her inch the sheet lower again. Her breasts were a dream, a fantasy. He kicked off his khakis, then removed his socks. Straightening, he dropped his fists onto his hips and just stood, letting her rake her gaze over him. "Darcy, it's a fact of life that a man can't fake his reaction to a woman. Look at me. Do I look like a man who doesn't appreciate the sight of your body?"

She boldly appraised him before shaking her head.

Leaving his underwear on—he didn't want to completely unnerve her—he slid into bed with her. Pulling her underneath him, he straddled her, gazing into her eyes. "Tell me you want this."

"I want this," she whispered.

"With me."

"With you."

He kissed her, trying to concentrate on his ultimate goal—her pleasure—and to ignore the need pulsing in him.

He suckled his way down her throat, pressing a kiss at its pounding base. "Don't forget, you have to tell me what you like."

"I like that."

"What?"

"Your lips on my skin."

He lowered his chest until their nipples met. Then he brushed back and forth until hers peaked.

Darcy gasped. "I...like that."

Michael smiled into her neck. Then he kissed his way down over her collarbone to her chest, and took her nipple in his mouth.

"Michael!" she said, jolting a little. "Oh, my!"

Michael cherished each breast in turn until Darcy was moving restlessly under him, her fingers tangled in his hair as she pressed him closer to her. He lost count how many times she breathed, "I like that," but each time he heard her say it, his desire peaked to a new level, until he wanted her more than he'd ever wanted anyone or anything in the world.

Cherishing Darcy was like cherishing life. Touching her, tasting her, licking her, was like reaching for the moon. Making her cry out her release would feel like conquering the universe.

While his thumbs continued brushing over her nipples, Michael moved lower. He nibbled on a hipbone, then licked the hollow. His teeth scraped lightly up her waist, then his tongue trailed down her center before jabbing lightly into her belly button.

"Oh, God, that's...good!"

Michael moved his knees between her thighs and nudged her legs apart. His hand whispered down her waist to her hipbone. "Open for me. Give it all to me, Darcy."

Her tense legs relaxed and she spread her thighs, gazing at him with such trust, he wanted to cry. He threaded his fingers through her soft mound. "Let yourself feel it, enjoy it. That's what this is all about, Darcy. Letting yourself go."

His thumb slowly circled lower until he found the center of her femininity. Darcy gasped and her legs started jerking.

But Michael didn't stop. "Picture yourself in a pool, the water sliding softly over your body, into your body, caressing you."

She was wet. Hot and wet. Hot and wet and ready to come. Michael slid his finger inside of her, stimulating her from without and within.

"That's wonderful," she gasped, her eyes closed, head thrown back. "Please, Michael!"

Her knees came up, clutching his hips. "Don't stop! Please, I don't want you to stop!"

Michael had no intention of stopping. Watching Darcy like this aroused him more than anything he'd ever witnessed in his life. The sense of rightness, of desire licking through him was the most powerful thing he'd ever felt.

She began shaking uncontrollably, her hands clutching and unclutching the bedsheet. Her head rolled from side to side, and she started chanting his name. Her hips pressed upward, silently begging for more. Michael gave it to her, knowing that at this moment he'd give her his life if she asked for it.

When he felt the first contractions of her muscles, he slid in and out of her faster, over her harder. When she screamed her climax, Michael almost came with her.

He drew it out, forcing her to experience every lurch of release, every wave of pleasure. When she finally sank back into the bed, when her legs went boneless, when her eyes opened and she stared at him in wonder, Michael slowed, then stopped. He leaned over her again, smiling down into her glistening eyes.

"Michael!" she breathed.

"Darcy!" he whispered back.

"That was...that was—"

"Did you like that?"

"Oh, yes!" she said, throwing her arms around his neck. "Oh, Michael! Show me how to do that to you."

He kissed her softly. "Not this time."

"But—"

"Darcy, all I want is to be inside of you. Me. My body."

"Yes, please."

He rolled to her side. "Take off my underwear, Darcy."

She complied with an eagerness that made his lust for her expand to record highs. She stared at him with unabashed curiosity. Michael leaned over her and grabbed a condom. Her hand circled his hard, needy shaft.

He sucked in a breath. "Easy, sweetheart," he groaned. "I'm just ready enough that if you touch me, I'll be spilling before I get near you."

"It's smooth."

"Uh-huh," he said, gritting his teeth. He hadn't counted on Darcy's need to explore new territory.

"And big. And hard."

Michael would bet it was harder than it had ever been in his life. Bigger, too. He gently disengaged her hand and rolled the condom into place. Then he took both her wrists and held them above her head with one hand. The other hand caressed her breast. "I want you so much," he whispered against her lips. "So damn much, Darcy."

"Take me."

His hand slid down her taut belly to her mound, and he started a slow, seductive arousal again. He wanted her as ready as him.

It didn't take long for him to get her writhing under his seduction. When he was near to exploding, he covered her body, spreading her legs. Looking deep into her eyes, he said, "I'm going to make love to you. If it hurts, I'm sorry. Just this once, all right?"

"Yes."

He kept his gaze locked with hers while he started to enter her. She was so slick and hot, her body accepting his invasion with surprising ease.

Her eyes went wide.

"Wrap your legs around me."

She did.

If there was still a barrier, Michael never felt it. But he knew the moment it began to hurt her, and he withdrew slowly. For an eternity, he merely entered a few inches and withdrew, letting her get used to the rhythm, the feeling of being possessed by a man. He kissed her, swallowing her occasional moan—of pleasure or pain, he wasn't certain.

Then Darcy did something that nearly shattered him. She clutched his hips with her legs, shifted a little, and thrust upward, burying him farther inside her.

Michael went still, trying to read her expression. Her eyes sparkled like gems in the soft candles' glow. "Am I hurting you?"

"No, no, not anymore. Please, Michael!"

That plea sounded as old as Eve's, and Michael lost all control. He put his hands under her shoulder blades and crushed her to him while he possessed her, over and over, plunging deep then withdrawing, again and again, until he was mindless.

Darcy's muscles contracted around him at the same time

she cried out. The joy of knowing that she'd experienced climax this way shot through him. He went over the edge, fast and hard. Pleasure burst through him, bathing him.

He hoarsely whispered his elation against her neck as he spilled and spilled and spilled out ecstasy.

He collapsed on her, his breaths rasping and harsh, his muscles turning fluid and useless. He'd never felt so utterly spent in his life.

And he'd never so desperately anticipated making love with a woman again.

When he finally found the energy to move, he withdrew from her and rolled onto his side, so filled with awe, he had no words to say. He pulled her into his arms, never wanting to let her go. If the force of a man's response to making love with a woman was any barometer, he was more than just physically attracted to Darcy Welham.

How much more, he refused to guess.

"I like sex," Darcy whispered in his ear.

He lifted his head and stared down at her. "I like sex, too. Especially with you."

"Really?"

He touched her cheek. "Darcy, what just happened to me has never happened to me before. That's the honest truth."

Her smile was beatific, angelic, and God help him, seductive all at once. He was lost. Completely lost.

"I'm glad," she said softly, threading her fingers through the hair on his chest. "Really glad."

"You're beautiful."

"You too."

"I never want this night to end."

"Same here. When do we get to do that again?"

Michael collapsed on his back. "I think I've just created a monster."

She giggled, then rolled to her side, draping her arm over his abdomen. "I have this gut instinct that tells me I still have a lot to learn. And you, Mr. Davidson, are going to teach me."

He groaned. "Did I ever tell you you're too smart for your own good?"

She kissed him. "It's my downfall."

"Darcy?"

"Hmm?" she said, exploring his ribs.

"I've changed my mind about something."

"What's that?"

"From now on, whenever you need to calm yourself down, I want you to picture the two of us making love. Because that was the most fantastic thing that's ever happened to me."

"Oh, Michael!" she cried, hugging him. "Thank you!"

"Darcy?"

"Yes?"

"I don't want this to end."

"Me either."

"Ever."

"DAVIDSON! Telephone," Tom Murphy boomed the next afternoon, striding into the kitchen where Michael was helping Darcy set up the salad bar. "Line one."

Michael sighed. He winked at Darcy. "Duty calls," he murmured, then brushed by her, letting his hand slide over her hip surreptitiously.

A delicious thrill jolted through Darcy and she nearly moaned. At the moment her body felt like it had been hit by an eighteen-wheeler sometime recently. She wouldn't have traded one wonderful ache for anything in the world.

She felt light as a cloud, and just as high in the sky. The night before would be one she treasured for the rest of her life.

She'd never felt more like a woman. Well-loved. Worshipped. Cherished. They'd hardly slept, as each took turns awakening the other to kiss, caress, make love. Sometimes they just held each other, whispering love words that made her heart soar and her body catch fire.

She was in love. Deeply, hopelessly in love.

Michael didn't want it to end. Ever. He'd said so. He

wasn't running away from her as other men had, but instead wanted to hold on to her and never let her go.

At dawn Michael had kissed her awake, then picked her up and carried her to her bathroom. He'd laid her gently into a perfectly heated bathtub full of bubbly water, then used a washcloth to soap every inch of her skin.

"This is paradise," she'd whispered sleepily, as the heat from the water seeped into her sore muscles and his hands massaged her gently.

He'd smiled that heart-melting smile she'd grown to adore, his hair rumpled like a little boy's. "I see a lot more paradise in our future, love."

Now, as she filled a vat with freshly made creamy garlic dressing, Darcy couldn't help but smile. Paradise. She'd found paradise.

Wendy Walker sidled up to her. "You seem awfully chipper today."

Darcy shrugged noncommittally. "How'd it go last night?"

Wendy tossed her head. "How'd what go?"

"Last I heard, you had big plans for a certain tall, dark and handsome executive type."

Wendy clucked, snapping stiff. "The jerk's gay." Then she walked away.

Darcy kept her hands moving, performing tasks. She kept her lips pressed together, silent. Because if she didn't, she was going to jump fifty feet in the air and scream with joy.

"DAVIDSON."

"Stella here, boss."

"Holding down the fort?" Michael asked his no-nonsense secretary.

"Trying. It's not easy with London breathing down my neck."

Michael's smile faded. Dick London was his boss. And his boss was not happy with Michael at the moment. He called almost daily to check on the Welham acquisition, and since Michael had little progress to report, the man was getting more and more strident.

"I'm sorry, Stell. He shouldn't be taking it out on you."

"You don't happen to have any good news I can pass along to the blowhard, do you?"

Michael sighed, propping his crossed ankles on Tom's desk. "Nope. The owner's daughter's still holding out."

"I have a suggestion."

"Shoot."

"Exactly."

"What?"

"Shoot her. Put us all out of our misery."

Michael laughed. "Can I let you in on a little secret, Stella?"

"Uh-oh. Why don't I think I'm going to like this?"

"I don't think I want this acquisition any longer."

There was a long pause. "It's worse than I thought. Why not?"

"Because the owner's daughter is proving to be a formidable opponent. I hate the idea of her losing."

"May I remind you of a couple of facts?"

"No."

"One, you're a barracuda," she went on, ignoring him.

"Flattery is good."

"We've climbed the ladder at a dizzying pace by you remembering that."

"I remember that."

"You're not acting barracuda-ish at the moment. Where's my hero who told me two weeks ago that he'd have this woman on her knees in a matter of days?"

Michael winced. He'd brought Darcy to her knees all right. In ways Stella could never imagine. "I misjudged her."

"Two, you never misjudge people."

"There's always a first for everything."

"Three, this is not the time for firsts."

Oh, yes it was. This was a time of plenty of firsts. "So my timing is off."

"Four, your timing is never off."

"Stella—"

"Five, couldn't you have waited to fall in love with her until after the papers were signed?"

Michael sat in stunned silence. Stella had always known him better than anyone save his mother and sister. She'd been with him since his first job as project supervisor, and had been—as far as he was concerned—as much a part of his success as he was.

But she was wrong this time. Michael wasn't in love with Darcy. He couldn't afford to be.

Stella sighed loudly into his ear. "I'm right, aren't I?"

He snorted. "Not hardly. I just find her..." What did he find Darcy? Attractive, certainly. Intriguing, definitely. Alluring, most assuredly. "Fascinating," he finished lamely.

"Michael, Michael, Michael. We've been together ten years. In that time I've seen hundreds of young ladies wiggle past you, trying to get even a speck of your attention. You never even noticed. I let you out of my sight for a few weeks, and look what you go and do."

"It's under control," he defended. "Jeez, I just sort of like her!"

"Shall I mention this little glitch to London?"

"If you want to get me fired, sure," he said mildly.

"Are you kidding? You're my meal ticket." She sighed again. "So what are we going to do?"

"We're going to broach the topic to Darcy one more time, and if she still says no, that's that."

"Darcy, is it?"

"It is."

"You don't strike me as the Darcy type."

"I'm definitely the Darcy type."

"You always went through Penelopes and Julianas and Moniques here in New York."

"In Washington, I go for Darcys."

"Do Darcys go for you?"

"In a big way," he boasted, feeling a swell of pride sweep through him.

"Maybe we can use this."

"No!" he barked swiftly, forgetting for the moment that this was his original plan. "I'm not using our personal relationship to get to her. No way."

"You're hooked like a catfish, buddy."

"No, I'm not. I just like her. I'm in control, I promise."

Stella grunted her disgust. "If you say so."

"Is there anything else, or are you going to lecture me some more?"

"Hmm. You've got about a million messages, but I'll take care of them here."

"Thank you."

"Oh, by the way, your sister called. She wants you to call her as soon as possible."

DARCY WAS FLOATING. Love had a profound effect, she decided. She hadn't made one mistake her entire shift, not one broken plate, not one spilled drink. She felt graceful and poised, happy and competent. Michael had given this to her. She would love him into eternity for that.

"What can I get you gentlemen?" she asked two businessmen, smiling.

They looked up from a ledger and both smiled back. She wanted to hug them. "What have you got, sweetheart?" the fat one asked, winking.

Darcy was too happy to take offense. "Anything on the menu, and whatever's behind that bar."

She felt, rather than saw, Michael approach. He took her arm. Looking at the customers, he said, "Please excuse us a moment," then nearly hauled her into the alcove where clean tableware was kept for the busboys.

She wondered if he'd heard the customer's suggestive question, but the expression on his face wasn't anger when she looked up at him. He appeared to be in pain.

"What's wrong?" she asked in a whisper.

"I have to fly back to New York, first thing in the morning."

"Why?"

"My mother's sick. I have to go see her."

"Oh, Michael, I'm sorry! Is it serious?"

He heaved a breath. "I don't know. She's been in the hospital for three days, and neither she nor my sister bothered to tell me. My sister said my mother didn't want me to worry. God, I'm going to kill them both when I get home."

"Well, maybe that's good. If she were really sick, your sister would have called right away."

"I don't care. They should have told me." He brushed a stray strand of her hair back over her shoulder. "I have to leave as soon as possible."

"Of course."

He took her arms. "Come with me."

"What?"

"I want you with me, Darcy. I need you with me. Please."

"I'll just be in the way."

"No, you won't. Besides, I want her to meet you." His eyes pleaded with her. His hands squeezed her, coaxing her. "Please."

11

DARCY HAD NEVER BEEN to New York City before, and truthfully, she didn't much care for it. Although overall the skyline was quite impressive, when one took in the scenery in small chunks, the city was absolutely squalid.

Since Michael grew up here, though, she didn't want to insult him. Therefore, as the taxi carted them from La Guardia to his town house, which he'd told her was located on the Upper East Side of Manhattan, she kept her opinion to herself.

They'd accomplished the trip north in relative silence, although they'd held hands for most of the plane ride. Michael seemed deep in thought, and Darcy decided to allow him his privacy, wanting just to be there if he needed her.

Somehow, by the way he looked at her occasionally, she sensed he appreciated it.

Darcy had never felt needed like this before. She hated the circumstances, but she loved that he wanted her near him for support. She looked over at him. He was writing on a large, yellow legal pad, a bouquet of flowers he'd bought from a vendor at La Guardia beside him. Feeling a little guilty, Darcy let her curiosity get the better of her, reading his bold, handwritten notes. Jeez, even his handwriting was sexy.

Suddenly she felt his eyes on her, and she looked up, a guilty flush inching up her throat. But he just smiled at her and took her hand.

"Thank you," he said, his voice low.

"For what?" She felt like she could drown in the blue of his eyes.

"For being here."

"There isn't anywhere else I'd rather be."

His smile was so gentle, Darcy felt weepy. But then it vanished, and a worried light came into his eyes. "Darcy, since I don't know what's wrong, I don't what we're going to encounter. It may not be pretty."

"Illness never is." She threaded their fingers. "It must be awful when it's someone you love."

He nodded, swallowing hard. Then, for some reason, he smiled. "Did I mention that I'm crazy about you?"

Darcy's jaw dropped and she slowly shook her head.

"I'm crazy about you."

Darcy had to fight not to blurt out how much she loved him. He hadn't used that word yet, and she felt foolish using it first. Especially if it might scare him off. Darcy had no idea what his feelings were on the subject of commitment. Yes, he'd said he didn't want what they had to end. He hadn't said he wanted that exclusively.

The thought of him having a relationship with another woman at the same time he had one with Darcy hurt terribly. But she had no right to make demands on him. On the other hand, feminine instinct told her that their lovemaking had affected him as deeply as he'd said. Maybe she'd be able to keep him so busy, he'd be too occupied with her even to *think* about other women. It was a very pleasurable thought. And it made her smile.

"I'm glad," she said softly. "Likewise."

"How do you like New York so far?"

"It's...big."

He laughed softly. "And ugly and dirty."

"I didn't say that."

"No, but you were thinking it, weren't you?"

"I'm sure parts of it are quite...clean."

He threw back his head and laughed. "Not many."

She looked out and realized they'd entered a more residential area. The houses were all but connected, and they did have small yards and a few lovely trees. It reminded her a little of Georgetown.

Still, she felt sorry for the children playing in their tiny yards that couldn't even hold a good-sized swing set.

Her children would never have tiny yards. Her children would have room to run and play. Her children would breathe fresh air.

Her children?

Darcy had never seriously considered the idea of having children before. She turned to look at Michael, who'd gone back to making notes. His nose was straight and strong, his chin solid. His eyelashes weren't really long, but they were thick, fringing the sparkling blue of his eyes. His pitch-black hair had just a hint of wave in it and was thick and silky.

Michael would produce beautiful children.

Darcy felt her biological clock start ticking.

"What are you staring at?" Michael asked her.

Darcy started. She had been staring, hadn't she? She blushed a little, but she answered him honestly. "You."

"That, I know. Why?"

"I just think you're beautiful."

"Hey!" he said with a mock frown. "Men can't be beautiful."

She ignored that. "Were you always so good-looking, or did you have to grow into it?"

He laughed nervously. "I have no idea."

"Do you look like your mother or your father?"

His laughter evaporated. "I don't look like my mother." He tapped his pencil against his legal pad. "Why all the questions?"

Darcy wasn't about to tell him she'd just decided she wanted her children to look like him. That wasn't possible, anyway. He was a New Yorker. His children would have a tiny yard and smoggy air.

She suddenly realized they'd come to a stop. Blessing the gods, she scrambled out of the cab without answering his question. Looking up, she gasped softly when she saw his home. It was really very pretty. No yard, of course. But still pretty.

After retrieving their bags and paying the cabbie, Michael joined her. "Like it?"

"Yes," she said, and smiled up at him. "Yes, I do."

"Good."

"Do you own it?" she asked as they headed up the walk.

"Me and the bank."

"It reminds me of the house on *The Cosby Show*."

Michael chuckled, transferring his duffel bag to beneath his left arm, then put his right hand on the small of her back and propelled her forward.

They walked up the steps while Darcy admired the intricately carved oak door with its big brass knocker. She also liked the crocks of colorful miniature snapdragons gracing either side of the doorway.

She looked up at Michael when they reached the entry. He, too, was gazing fondly at the flowers. He dropped the bags and reached in his pants pocket, smiling down at her. Nodding at the plants, he said, "At least that's a good sign. My mother has a thing for flowers."

So that's where he got it, huh? Darcy would bet a lot of money that Michael used to bring his mother flowers all the time when he was growing up.

Michael took a small set of keys from his pocket, but to Darcy's surprise, he jabbed the doorbell three times—and three bursts of short buzzing noises sounded behind the door. He unlocked it and waved her in.

"Why'd you do that?" Darcy asked, after he'd followed her. She looked around. The foyer was lovely, with a green marble floor, and brass planters containing potted palms.

Ah, yes, and a thing for plants, too.

Michael shrugged. "That's our signal. We always announce we're home that way, so when one of us hears the front door opening, we know right away it's not a burglar."

Sure enough, a squeal sounded from the back of the house. And someone came pounding down the long, narrow hallway. "Michael!"

A lovely young woman came out of the shadows and hurled herself at him. All Darcy registered were long bare

legs and a long black ponytail before Michael chuckled and
twirled the girl around. She sure hoped this was his sister.

When Michael finally set her back on her feet, the girl
started checking him over, as if searching for signs of in-
jury. While she examined him, she talked. Faster than
Darcy had heard anyone talk in her life.

"So glad you're home, even though it wasn't really nec-
essary. Mother's much better today. She's so happy to be
home from the hospital. Doc Forsner's up with her now,
so we'll know more shortly. Are you home for good? We
really miss you. You have about a zillion messages on the
machine. I swear, that Diana Prescott is one persistent
woman. She refused to believe you didn't want her to rush
down to D.C. and keep you—"

The woman would have continued, but Michael prevented it by slapping a hand over her mouth. He turned her
slowly to face Darcy. "Darcy, meet Anne Elizabeth Davidson. She has a vivid imagination and a very big mouth.
Annie, this is Darcy. Darcy also has a vivid imagination—"
at that he gave Darcy a very knowing leer over his sister's
head "—but she knows how to keep her mouth shut."

Blue eyes that mirrored Michael's went wide. Except that
she looked several years younger than her brother, they
could have been twins. And somehow, strangely, the features that looked so masculine on Michael looked exactly
the opposite on his sister. She looked to be about three or
four inches shorter than Darcy, but still fairly tall. And
lovely.

Michael slowly peeled his hand from Anne's mouth. It
had formed a small O.

"Say hello to Darcy, Annie."

"Hello, Darcy."

Despite the fact that the name Diana Prescott was still
ringing in Darcy's ears, she couldn't help but smile. "Hi,
Annie."

Annie grinned as she glanced from Darcy to Michael.
"Well, well, well."

A look passed between brother and sister that Darcy

didn't understand. Annie's expression seemed to say, "I've got a secret." Michael's seemed to say, "Shut up, Annie."

Darcy broke the thick silence. "I'm glad to hear your mother's feeling better."

Annie looked back at her. "She'll feel a whole lot better when she sees Michael." She paused. "And you." She cocked her head. "Anyone ever tell you you look like Grace Kelly?"

Michael shot Darcy an I-told-you-so look.

Darcy rolled her eyes. "Does this family have a Grace Kelly fetish?"

"Yes," Michael and Annie said at the same time. But Annie elaborated. "Well, my mother does, at any rate. When we were growing up, she'd make an event out of watching a Grace Kelly movie. My mother always loved her because the first thing my father said to her when he met her was, 'Did anyone ever tell you you look like Grace Kelly?' So she felt this—"

"Enough, Annie," Michael interrupted.

Darcy almost choked on her outrage. Michael had used the same line on her that his deserting rat of a father had used on his vulnerable mother? He was going to hear about that.

The nervous gleam in his eyes told her he realized that. "Annie, why don't you take Darcy to the kitchen and get her some iced tea or something. I'm going to take our suitcases upstairs, then look in on Mom."

"Sure!" Annie said, her smile friendly, curious and just a little mischievous.

"And keep your mouth shut," Michael warned. "Or talk about your writing."

With that he winked at Darcy and started up the stairs.

They both watched him go, then looked at each other. Annie said, "Do *you* want me to keep my mouth shut?"

"I want you to tell me everything."

"Good."

As MICHAEL descended the steps, he heard Darcy's laughter, and his heart lurched a little. Why, he didn't know. He supposed he just liked hearing her happy.

Why had he been so desperate to have Darcy with him? It was a question he did and didn't want to probe. Admitting that he wanted her with him didn't bother him. Admitting that he *needed* her with him did.

Shaking his head, he buried the questions for now. Heading down the hallway, he heard his sister say, "Senior Vice President!"

Uh-oh.

Michael hightailed it into the kitchen, just as Darcy said, "That's wonderful! He never told me that."

They were seated at the picnic-style kitchen table, built into a nook in the corner. Darcy's back was to him. Annie started to open her mouth, but shut it when she caught Michael's glare.

Darcy turned, and Michael quickly masked his expression. Her eyes were so filled with pride, he felt guilt wash through him. If she knew what his promotion hinged on, that look of pure admiration and pride would die a very, very quick death.

"I thought I told you to talk about your writing," Michael said, forcing a grin.

Annie waved. "We did. That took all of five minutes."

Michael poured himself a glass of iced tea from the pitcher sitting on the counter, squeezed a slice of lemon into it, then moved to the table. Darcy immediately scooted over on the bench, and Michael sat down beside her.

His hand automatically sought her thigh. For some reason, touching Darcy had become an imperative to him. Last night, when they were in her bed, exhausted from making love, he'd pulled her into his arms and instantly fallen asleep, contentment, fulfillment and a sense of rightness blanketing him.

When he'd awakened in the middle of the night, Darcy no longer in his arms, a feeling of panic, of loss, had gripped him. In the darkness of the room, he couldn't see Darcy, but then she shifted in bed and uttered a little, soft sigh. Michael had moved closer to her and tucked her back into his arms, then had immediately fallen back asleep, his world restored.

Amazingly enough, that was a first for him. Michael had never cared to share a bed for any reason besides sex. He supposed that meant it was going to take longer before he started getting that bored sensation that marked the end of all of his relationships.

"Why didn't you tell me you were up for a promotion?" Darcy asked him.

Michael shrugged. "The subject never came up." With good reason.

Annie gave him a quizzical look, but she knew better than to pursue the subject. "How's Mom?"

Michael frowned. "She's got a kidney infection, that's how she is. And I should have been told about it immediately."

"We didn't want you to worry. The doctor said it was minor and could be treated with antibiotics."

Michael's scowl could turn wine into vinegar. Annie withstood it quite nicely, however. Her smile remained angelic. "Did you tell Mother that Darcy's here?"

Michael nodded. "That perked her right up," he said dryly.

"I had the feeling it would," Annie chirped.

"Why?" Darcy asked.

Before Michael could stop her, Annie grabbed at the bit and ran with it. "Because Michael's never brought a woman home to meet our mother in his life. Mom's been fretting for years that he'd never get married because he didn't care enough about any of his girlfriends to bring them home. She always says—"

"Enough, Annie."

"—the first girl to walk through our front door would be the one who—"

"Annie!"

"—steals Michael's heart," Annie finished quickly.

Michael closed his eyes, sifting through his options for

silencing his sister permanently. She didn't realize the damage she was causing. He didn't want Darcy getting false hopes. Although at the moment he couldn't imagine not having Darcy in his life, he knew that eventually they'd part ways. He just wasn't a permanent-type guy.

Okay, so in the afterglow of incredible lovemaking, he'd surprised himself by telling her he never wanted what they had to end. What he'd meant was the great sex they'd enjoyed together.

Hadn't he?

He opened his eyes and glared at his sister, who smiled sweetly at him, then returned her attention to Darcy. "And believe me, I've double-dated with Michael a few times—"

"Annie."

"You should see the mannequin types he's considered acceptable dating material."

"Annie."

"Cool, sophisticated, *boring*."

"Annie!"

Michael felt Darcy stiffen beside him.

"I'm certainly not cool or sophisticated," she said glumly.

He resisted the urge to put a reassuring arm around her. Glaring his displeasure at his sister, who densely didn't seem to realize she was hurting Darcy, not helping her, he squeezed Darcy's leg.

"Exactly!" Annie cried triumphantly. "You're real. Flesh and blood."

Michael looked at Darcy, almost in a new light. His sister had known her for all of thirty minutes, and she'd actually pinpointed what *was* different about Darcy from his usual taste in women. She *was* real. She *was* all creamy flesh and red-hot blood. And suddenly he realized his taste had undergone a drastic change. He couldn't imagine, now, why he'd wasted so many nights with Diana Prescott, a woman who loved clothes, jewelry and herself, not necessarily in that order.

The only jewelry Darcy ever wore were earrings, an emerald ring and an occasional bracelet. Her clothes were nice, but casual. She looked good in them, but then again, she could look good in the proverbial burlap sack. And if Darcy had any problems, being in love with herself was not one of them.

Michael felt an intense rush of desire for the woman beside him. His hand tightened on her leg as he tried to fight it. No matter how enticing the prospect, dragging Darcy upstairs now would likely embarrass her.

Michael searched his brain for a subject that would cool off his raging hormones. None came to mind. All roads led to Darcy—in his arms, in his bed.

While images bloomed, Michael became vaguely aware that the conversation between Darcy and Annie had continued without him. He tried to concentrate on the words they uttered, but to no avail. He was too busy with his fantasies.

Darcy couldn't quite figure out what was wrong with Michael. He seemed lost in thought. She supposed worry over his mother preoccupied him. She wished there was some way she could ease the strain, get his taut body to relax. Only one way came to mind. She blushed at the scandalous thought. Now was not the time to be thinking of sex.

Unfortunately, when she looked at Michael, she couldn't think of much else. In two short nights, Michael had awakened something in her, and Darcy didn't want it to go back to sleep. Ever.

"So he got a paper route and also worked for old Mrs. Whitley after school. Jeez, even back then he was taking care of us."

Darcy dragged her attention back to Annie. If she assimilated this conversation correctly, Annie was listing Michael's attributes. Annie didn't really need to do that. Darcy already loved the man more than life. Still, she liked hearing affirmation that she'd fallen in love with Mr. Right.

She smiled. Michael was so lost in thought, she didn't think he even realized they were discussing him unashamedly. "Who's Diana Prescott?"

Even that didn't yank him back to reality. One of his hands toyed with the rim of his glass, the other rhythmically squeezed and released her thigh.

Annie waved. "Don't worry about her. He's bored with her already. All the signs say so. He didn't even want her to know where he was staying in D.C."

Darcy's smile vanished. "Does he bore easily?"

"Until now, yes. I think that's all about to change."

"Why?" Darcy whispered. "To tell you the truth, I'm fairly new to the dating game."

"Get out!" Annie said. "You're beautiful!"

"I'm a disaster waiting to happen."

Annie's expression softened at Darcy's admission. "Mike's pretty good at building dreams out of disasters. It's what he does best."

Mike? Darcy rolled the nickname over her tongue. She liked it. She started to say something else, but shuffling footsteps stopped her. She looked over her shoulder. A distinguished older gentleman appeared at the entry to the kitchen, a black bag in his hand.

Annie stood. Darcy shook Michael's arm and he blinked twice before his eyes seemed to clear and he focused on her face. For some reason he flushed a little.

"The doctor," Darcy mumbled.

Michael stood and turned. "What's the verdict?"

"She'll be fine," the doctor said. "Just make sure she takes her medication until it's gone. And I want to see her again in ten days. Sooner, if she doesn't show signs of steady improvement. Keep an eye on her."

"We will," Michael and Annie said at the same time.

Michael shook the doctor's hand. "Doc, this is Darcy Welham. Darcy, Doc Forsner, the only doctor in the country who still makes house calls."

The doctor chuckled. "Only for my special patients," he said. "Laura and I went to school together. Nice to meet you Ms. Welham."

Annie suddenly turned wide eyes on Darcy. "Welham? But—"

"Thanks again, Doc," Michael interrupted her. "Is she still awake?"

"Wide-awake and feisty as ever."

Annie was still gaping at Darcy, but she didn't have time to think through her reaction. Michael turned to her. "Will you come meet my mother?"

"I'd be honored."

DARCY'S NERVES fluttered as she took a look at Michael one final time before entering his mother's bedroom. He smiled down at her, encouraging her. Fortified, she stepped over the threshold into the room.

She'd never been introduced to a man's mother before. Not in the role of the man's current girlfriend, at any rate. She desperately wanted to make a good impression on Mrs. Davidson. She felt certain that his mother's opinion meant everything to him. And therefore, her.

The room was large and airy, obviously the master bedroom. Darcy thought that was sweet, that Michael had given his mother the best bedroom in his house.

Expecting his mother to be in bed, Darcy was surprised that the thick, white comforter was pulled up and colorful pillows littered the head artlessly. The wallpaper was a light floral print, matching the lacy curtains at the windows.

Two sea-green chaise longues flanked a small fireplace. Sitting in one, a light blanket covering her legs, was Michael's mother, knitting and humming at once.

Darcy's first reaction was shock at how petite the woman was. Darcy would bet she stood no taller than five feet, and would only top a hundred pounds if she wore a soaking-wet snowsuit and carried a ten-pound bowling ball.

Her hair was the pure white of a woman who had once been blond, artfully rolled in a bun. Her features were as delicate as her bone structure, and if she had dyed her hair, she could passed for a woman in her early forties.

She stopped humming, so the snick of her knitting needles was the only sound in the room. Some instinct must have warned her of their entry, because she looked up over her half glasses. And smiled.

She was radiant, almost ethereal, and Darcy was struck mute and immobile by the glow that seemed to surround Michael's mother.

"Oh! You must be Darcy," she said, taking off her glasses and setting her knitting aside.

"Don't get up, Mother," Michael said, giving Darcy a gentle shove toward the fireplace.

"Nonsense," his mother retorted, tossing off the blanket and rising. She wore a lovely bright-blue-and-red sweater and a pair of red wool slacks. On her feet were bunny slippers.

Feeling like an amazon, Darcy approached her, and accepted the tiny hand Mrs. Davidson extended to her.

"Welcome, Darcy," his mother said, beaming. She made no effort to hide her curiosity as she took in every inch of Darcy.

Embarrassed that she'd dressed for comfort rather than appearances, Darcy smiled. She couldn't help it. Not when the woman's gray-green eyes were so filled with serene pleasure.

"I'm happy to be here, ma'am."

"None of this ma'am stuff. Michael, tell her none of this ma'am stuff."

"None of this ma'am stuff," Michael repeated obediently.

Darcy looked at him, at the adoration glowing in his eyes as he smiled at his mother, and she felt a twinge of envy. She wanted, more than anything in the world, for him to look at her like that.

"Michael, be a dear and bring Darcy and me something to drink, please," Mrs. Davidson said.

Darcy knew a dismissal when she heard one. She looked at Michael, panicked. "I...if I have any more tea, I'll float home to D.C."

His mother laughed softly. "I'm not really thirsty, either. So, just scram, Michael."

Darcy looked into those gray eyes. They looked wise and warm, and Darcy relaxed.

"Are you trying to get rid of me, Mother?" Michael asked.

"You always were an astute boy," his mother said, patting his hand. "Get."

In a nervous fog, Darcy accepted a reassuring kiss on the cheek from Michael, then watched him stroll out of the room, whistling. Turning back to his mother, she smiled tentatively, clasping her hands together to keep them from shaking.

"Sit, Darcy," Mrs. Davidson said, waving at the second lounge chair.

Darcy obeyed immediately, then fidgeted a little while Mrs. Davidson made herself comfortable. Darcy had a hard time conceiving of this tiny woman producing a big hulk of a man like Michael. His father must have been a giant.

A long silence ensued while Mrs. Davidson looked Darcy over in detail. Then suddenly she smiled. "Michael didn't exaggerate. You're quite beautiful."

Darcy's heart fluttered. It was one thing to hear a man tell her she was beautiful when she knew he was trying to seduce her. It was another to hear that he shared that view with his mother. "Thank you. So are you."

Mrs. Davidson laughed. "Oh, I'm just an old lady."

Darcy shook her head. "No." She couldn't stop herself from blurting out the thoughts whirling in her head. "But you're so tiny! How did you ever manage to carry Michael, Mrs. Davidson?"

Her laughter tinkled through the room. It was light and airy. "Please, call me Laura." Absently, she took up her needles and began knitting again, as if she couldn't bear to sit idle. "Michael was only a little bigger than the average infant at birth. But he made up for it rather quickly. He had to learn to walk early, because I certainly couldn't carry him for long." Her eyes paled a little with what Darcy thought was sadness. "Michael had to learn a lot of things much earlier than he should have had to."

Darcy had no idea how to respond to that. Her cheeks warmed. She felt uncomfortable knowing the details of this woman's life.

Mrs. Davidson sighed. "Has Michael told you about his childhood?"

"Just bits and pieces. He told me how much you did for him."

Peering over her glasses, Mrs. Davidson frowned. "He's still spouting that nonsense, is he?"

"Well," Darcy said, wondering why that seemed to consternate the older woman. "He's grateful."

"It's hogwash, you know. I only did what any mother would have done."

"He seems to think," Darcy said quietly, "that you sacrificed your life for his."

Mrs. Davidson's knitting dropped to her lap, and she clucked in disgust. "I should box that boy's ears."

Darcy stifled a giggle. Michael's mother would need a ladder to reach his ears.

The woman clucked again. "My children *are* my life. I can't believe he's still carrying around all that baggage. What utter nonsense."

"Nonsense?"

Mrs. Davidson laughed. "Darcy, did Michael happen to tell you anything else about his childhood, other than the fact that his mother was some sort of martyred saint?"

Darcy smiled at the mirth in those gray eyes. Happy to hear any and everything about Michael, she shook her head.

"You might have noticed that Michael is...hmm, somewhat organized?"

Darcy snorted. "He could give lessons to the military."

Michael's mother nodded, grinning. "He has been like that since he was in diapers. Even before he could write, he kept inventory of his toys."

Mrs. Davidson took up her knitting. "He would travel down to the toy store and pick out something he just *had* to have. He'd calculate down to the penny how much more money he needed than he had saved to buy it. Then he'd walk up and down the street, offering to do chores for the neighbors in exchange for pennies, nickels, quarters.

"As soon as he earned enough money, he'd march down to the toy store and buy that precious toy. Inevitably, he'd see something else he wanted, so the cycle started all over again."

Mrs. Davidson paused, then smiled sadly. "After…his father left, all of that changed. He never once set his sights on a toy again. Instead, he'd see that there were holes in Annie's socks, so he'd earn money to buy her new ones. The toaster would break, and within a week, he'd buy a replacement."

Darcy ached for the little boy who'd had to go from nurtured to nurturing overnight. She ached for the man who carried the weight of guilt for so many things beyond his control.

"The only luxury he spent his money on was flowers."

Darcy looked up sharply. "Flowers?"

"Flowers," Mrs. Davidson repeated, pointing to the bouquet Michael had bought at the airport. "He knew how much I loved flowers. Once a week, like clockwork, I'd get flowers from him. Sometimes, when he didn't have the money, he'd pilfer flowers from the park. I could always tell when he'd had to go searching for them."

Mrs. Davidson shook her head, then held up her knitting to survey it. "By the time Michael was ten, he was a workaholic. He was never satisfied. Every time he accomplished a goal, he looked around wildly for another one to take its place. Then he'd come home and proudly announce what was next on his plate."

"God, I love this man," Darcy whispered under her breath.

Apparently, there was nothing wrong with Mrs. Davidson's hearing. She lowered her knitting. "I'm glad to hear it. Maybe you can be the one to get him to stop chasing titles and start chasing children."

Darcy snapped stiff. "Please, Mrs. Davidson, don't pin your hopes on me. Michael hasn't mentioned anything about commitment, much less marriage or children. I…think he was just lonely in Washington, and I…was convenient. Pretty soon he'll be returning to New York and he'll be busy with his new job… and—''

His mother's brows furrowed. ''New job?''

''Oh! Oh, I'm sorry, maybe he was saving the good news until he actually got named senior vice president.''

''No, I knew about it. But he told me, not an hour ago, not to count on it. As if I care whether he runs the whole country, just so long as he's happy.''

Darcy stopped tracing the seams on the chair. ''He found out he's not getting the promotion?''

Laura shrugged. ''Not exactly. Apparently, this big deal he's been working on down in Washington isn't going to go through.''

''The deal in Washington?'' Darcy croaked. ''What does that have to do with it?''

''He said when he comes back empty-handed, he'll be lucky to keep his job. He's exaggerating, probably. Michael always lands on his feet. But I know how much he hates to fail, and I'm sure he'll consider that a failure. So you just make sure to be there to comfort him.'' With that, she laughed.

DARCY QUIETLY closed Mrs. Davidson's door behind her, then walked to the staircase. There she stopped and gripped the railing, taking deep, steadying breaths.

Michael's promotion, maybe even his job, depended on the restaurant deal. The stakes were that high. And he'd never even told her that.

Why hadn't he told her that? Was it pride? Or something more sinister? It hurt terribly, but she'd be a fool not to consider the possibility. Was Michael using her? Making her fall in love with him so that he could manipulate her into giving her father the go-ahead? Was he that much of a conniving bastard?

After all, just the way he talked about his family made

it clear that they came first with him. He'd do anything for them. Would he do this?

Darcy tried to think. When had Michael started showing interest in her? It seemed like he'd been around about three weeks. Soon after her father had come to town.

Her father. What had her father told him? Had he told Michael she had the final say? Probably. Which of course would explain Michael's sudden turnaround. And the rea-son he hadn't mentioned the takeover to her for quite a while. He'd wanted to soften her up first.

No, she wouldn't believe that. Even if he'd started out trying to soften her, he wasn't faking his feelings now, was he? If so, he deserved an Oscar.

Her mind was jumbled, her insides shaking from the thought that any or all of these possibilities were based in fact. If so, her heart was about to be shattered.

Somehow, she had to find a way to ask Michael about what she'd learned. She desperately hoped he had a reasonable explanation. Like that he'd fallen madly in love with her, couldn't live without her, and would she please marry him and bear him two-point-five children.

Darcy made her way down the steps, her heart pounding. She didn't know how she was going to ask him without making an utter fool of herself. But she had to know, before she invested any more emotional capital in him.

As she started down the hall to the kitchen, she heard the murmur of voices, one male, one female. Michael's angry "No!" brought Darcy up short.

"But, Michael, I can't live off you forever. Until I make a sale, I think I should go to work."

"You *are* working. Your writing is your work."

"My writing is my dream."

"That's even more reason. I'm not going to let you give up on your dream."

"You are such a pain!"

"Thank you very much."

"What happens if you *do* lose your job?" Annie said softly.

Darcy wasn't an eavesdropper by nature, but at the moment she couldn't force herself to move, to make a sound that would alert them to her presence.

"I'll get another paper route," Michael said dryly.

"Be serious!"

"I sincerely doubt that will happen, Annie-bell. So stop worrying your little head over it."

"Why don't you just tell Darcy the problem? Maybe she'll agree—"

"No! Absolutely not!"

"Mike, I think she really cares. If she knew your predicament—"

"I said no," he interrupted again, his voice like steel. "You have your dreams and Darcy has hers. I'd no more ask her to give up her dream because of me than I'd ask you. We'll find a way, Annie. Trust me, please."

"When are you going to stop promoting everyone else's dream and start working on your own?"

"Quit being so dramatic, Annie. I'm doing just fine."

"What about Darcy?"

"What about her?"

"Do you...like her?"

Darcy tensed, waiting for his answer.

"Yeah, Annie-bell, I do. A lot."

"I do too."

"Good."

"She's nothing like your usual girlfriends."

Michael chuckled. "You know what's funny about that? I think that's exactly why I like her."

Darcy slumped against the wall, both elated and frightened. A man had never professed to really liking her before. A man had never cared more about her dream than his. A man had never meant so much to her. Of course, he hadn't mentioned love. But she was just optimistic enough to hope they would progress to that part.

And in that moment, Darcy knew what she had to do.

12

THAT NIGHT, Darcy dreamt of her mother. It was the summer of Darcy's seventh year, and she and her mother were enjoying a rare afternoon together. They'd gone to see a Disney movie, which had made Darcy cry because an animal had died in it.

Afterward, her mother took her to Baskin-Robbins. They carried their cones to the park across the street, and sat in the warm noon sun.

Darcy licked a drop of chocolate ice cream from her hand. "What happens to animals when they die?"

"They go to heaven, just like people do, Darcy. God loves all of his creatures."

"If he loves us, why does he let us die?"

"Because he wants us with him, eventually."

"I don't want you to go be with him. I want you to stay with me."

Her mother hugged her. "I plan on staying with you for a long, long time, baby."

The image melted, and another took its place. Darcy stood in her family's large country kitchen, her shoulders shaking with her sobs. Luli, their housekeeper, was hugging her, trying to comfort her. "Now, sugar, your mama's gotta do what she gotta do."

"She promised she'd be here for my birthday."

Just then her mother entered, looking harried and hurried. Darcy turned her head the other way and let out a loud wail.

Her mother took her shoulders and turned her around. "Oh, honey, you know I wouldn't go if I didn't have to."

She pushed Darcy's hair out of her face. "When I get back we'll have the biggest party you've ever seen."

"You love the restaurants more than me."

"No! That's not true! Why do you think I'm doing this, Darcy? For me? No. This is for you, for your future."

"I don't want them. I hate them."

Her mother shook her slightly. "Don't ever say that! These restaurants will be your legacy someday. We're working hard to build a dream, Darcy. For you. Because we love you so much."

Darcy tried to smile, but her lips trembled. "When will you be home?"

"Just as soon as I can. I promise."

But Darcy's mother never kept that promise.

Darcy whimpered in her sleep, but before she had time to dwell on the fate of her mother, the dream shifted again.

Michael loomed over her, whispering her name.

"Michael," she replied brokenly. "Hold me."

She felt his comforting weight, smelled his masculine scent so deeply, she could almost believe he was really there.

"I'm here, Darcy. I'm not going anywhere."

"She died trying to build a dream for me."

Warm lips brushed over hers. "I know, love."

A sigh escaped her. Then a hand covered her breast over the cotton of her nightshirt. Darcy's eyes flew open, and she nearly screamed when she realized there really was someone in bed with her.

The scream died when she saw Michael's sleep-groggy eyes and tousled hair above her. "Michael?"

"You were expecting someone else?" he asked, arching an eyebrow.

Darcy tried to get her bearings. "You shouldn't be here. We're in your mother's house!"

"We're in *my* house, and there's nowhere I should be more."

He buried his head in the hollow that connected her shoulder to her neck. "I couldn't stay away."

Propriety aside, Darcy was thrilled he'd come. She'd retired to the guest room reluctantly around midnight, feeling bereft. Having Michael under the same roof but not in the same bed held no appeal whatsoever. But she hadn't wanted to make a bad impression, so she'd insisted on them sleeping in separate rooms.

She'd spent a wonderfully pleasant evening with his family. First Michael barbecued steaks, and after she and Annie cleaned up, the four of them played Scrabble, Michael cheating outrageously.

When Laura began to get tired, Michael had cut short the game and escorted her upstairs. When he returned, the three of them talked and sipped wine for another two hours, then Darcy had excused herself—one of Annie's manuscripts in hand—to give Michael and his sister time alone.

But now he was here, holding her, exploring her neck with his lips and her breasts with his hand, and Darcy couldn't have kicked him out if her life depended on it.

Ribbons of desire streaked from her puckered breasts to her very center and she moaned softly. "Michael..."

"Tell me," he whispered against her throat. "Tell me."

"Undress me."

He chuckled softly. "With pleasure."

And pleasure was what he proceeded to give her.

Afterwards, instead of collapsing on her as he usually did, he tightened his hold on her head and gazed at her so hotly, he reminded her of an unleashed beast.

"Michael?" she said, not really frightened, just dazed by the power of what had just happened to her.

"I can't get enough of you," he whispered, his breaths still coming fast and shallow. He withdrew from her and rolled to his back, then grabbed her waist and pulled her to him.

Elation was a mild word for how Darcy felt. This man—this handsome, strong, caring, smart, successful man—couldn't get enough of her. Another first at the hands of Michael Stephen Davidson.

Darcy lay in the circle of Michael's strong, warm embrace and realized that life as she knew would never be the same. She was the luckiest woman on the face of the earth. "Michael?" she whispered, snuggling even closer.

His arms tightened around her. "Hmm?"

"Thank you."

A chuckle rumbled in his chest, against her ear. "For what?"

"For...everything."

He chuckled again. "Happy to oblige."

"WHAT THE HELL is this?"

Darcy looked up from the sandwich she was eating after her shift. Michael stood in the doorway to the break room, looking like a dark, angry, vibrating male. In his hand was Darcy's letter of resignation.

"Exactly what it looks like. My two weeks' notice."

They'd arrived back in D.C. last night, and had gone directly to Darcy's apartment. By unspoken agreement, they both knew Michael would spend the night. And he had. An incredible night in which he'd laid back and let Darcy direct their lovemaking.

He'd left at ten in the morning to go to his hotel and change. Right after he'd gone, Darcy had made one phone call, typed one letter, then showered, changed and came to work.

"I know what it is. What I want to know is why."

She shrugged. "You yourself told me I wasn't cut out for this business."

"Darcy—"

Tom popped his head in the door. "Telephone, Davidson. Ed Welham, line two."

Michael opened his mouth, then shut it again. Jeez, he looked good in blue. Of course, he looked good in gray, too, come to think of it. And in khaki. And in nothing at all. Especially in nothing at all.

He pointed at her nose. "This conversation's not over with. Don't you move your pretty little butt from that chair. I'll be right back."

Darcy squelched the desire to run from the restaurant like a frightened rabbit. She had the feeling he'd have a whole lot more to talk about after this phone call.

He'd told her on the plane home that he'd have to head back to New York after seeing her safely back to D.C. He hadn't said so, but the message was implicit. He'd decided to stop pursuing the Welham acquisition, and he had no reason to stay in Washington. He had to return to his office and face the music.

Darcy hadn't wanted to get into a discussion about it on the plane, so she'd failed to mention the decision she'd made in New York. Well, it looked like they were about to get into a discussion about it real soon.

The club sandwich suddenly didn't look so appealing. She didn't know how Michael would react to the news that Welham's was once again on the block. He was a proud man, and she worried that he'd consider her change of heart as a handout of some sort.

She heard the angry click of shoes against the tile floor in the kitchen, striding in her direction, and for a moment contemplated running out the back door. Trying to appear casual, she toyed with her pickle and studied the mound of chips on her plate.

He didn't say a word. Instead, he just took her arm and hauled her out of her chair. Silently he dragged her out the door to the back parking lot and shoved her into the passenger seat of his latest rental car. As he stomped around the front of the convertible, he glared through the windshield at her.

Definitely, he was not a happy camper.

He slid into the driver's seat and slammed the door shut with enough force to make Darcy jump. Popping the steering wheel up and out of his way, he turned to her. "Well?"

Darcy batted her eyelashes. "Well…what?"

"Don't play games with me, Darcy. I'm not in the mood."

"Tell me what's wrong and I'll see if I can't fix it."

He took a breath that said, *Lord, grant me patience.* "Why did you change your mind about the takeover?"

"What makes you think I changed my mind?"

His eyes blazed. "Dammit, Darcy, don't do this," he growled. "Just tell me what the hell is going on."

She clasped her hands together. "I changed my mind."

Michael swore explosively. "Why? Why would you change your mind? This is your *dream,* dammit!"

Shaking her head adamantly, she said, "No, it's not."

His jaw dropped.

Darcy took his hands and gazed into his eyes. "I've been doing a lot of thinking, lately." She nodded toward the restaurant. "This isn't my dream and never has been. It was my mother's dream."

"But—"

"No. Just listen. All my life I've been reliving my mother's last words to me, and taking them literally. She told me she and my father were working so hard because the restaurants were my future. To me that had always meant that I was destined to take over the restaurants. But that's not what she meant at all. She meant that the success of the restaurants would help ensure that I'd be able to do what I wanted with my future. That I'd have choices." She squeezed his hands. "They were a means to an end. And I'm ready to let them go and get on with what I really want to do with my life."

Michael swallowed. "And what is that?"

It was her turn to swallow. "Professionally, I'm not certain." She lowered her gaze to their entwined hands, swallowed one more time, and took the plunge. "Personally, I just want you in my life."

"Darcy—"

"Wait! Let me finish while I still have the courage." She lifted her chin and met his gaze. "I'm not asking anything of you, I'm really not. Except that you keep in touch with me. Maybe come and visit me once in a while."

He pulled his hands from hers and Darcy had a momentary twinge of panic. But instead of withdrawing from her, he took her shoulders and gave her a hard stare. "Are you sure about this? Really sure?"

"Yes," she whispered.

"You're not doing this for me, are you? I'd never forgive myself if you gave up on your dream for me."

"No," she lied. Well, half lied. She was doing it for all of them. For Michael, for his mother, for his sister, for her father, for herself. "I want this. I really do."

He was silent while his gaze penetrated hers, searching, she felt certain, for signs of deceit. "You won't regret it?"

"No." She sighed. "It'll be a relief, actually."

"I'm going to be real honest here, all right?"

Darcy's heart chilled with fear. "Yes."

"I'm not going to pretend this isn't really good news for me. But if there's even a small part of you that doesn't want to do this, please put a stop to it now and think about it for a while. It's a huge decision. And I don't want you making it for any reason except you're certain it's what you want. Because there's no going back, Darcy.

"If there's any part of you doing this for me, don't do it. I'm hoping we have a really great future together. And by the way, it's going to include a whole lot more than an occasional visit. But there are no guarantees. And if something happens between you and me, I can't live with you regretting the decision because you made it on my behalf." His fingers dug into the flesh of her upper arms. "Make sure this is the best decision for *you.*"

Darcy thought she loved Michael more in this moment than it was possible to love a man. And she knew in that moment that she *was* doing it for herself. For her future with him. "This is the best decision for me."

Amazingly, his eyes got a little misty. "You're sure?"

"I'm sure."

He yanked her against him and kissed her. Passionately. Hotly. Thoroughly. Long minutes later he broke the kiss and rested his forehead on hers. "If that's the case, I'll have to leave for Spokane tomorrow."

"I suspected as much."

"Come with me."

"I can't."

"Why not?"

"I'm already scheduled to work a private party Thursday night."

"To hell with that."

She pulled back. "Michael, I gave notice, and I have every intention of fulfilling my obligation to this company until such time as my employment is terminated. I owe that much."

He heaved a breath. "I'm going to miss you."

"You'll be too busy to miss me."

He shook his head. "I'll probably sit through contract negotiations daydreaming about tonight."

"Tonight?"

He grinned. "Tonight."

"What about tonight?"

"Our celebration."

"What celebration?"

"The one we're going to have tonight."

She sighed in exasperation. "What are you talking about? Are we going out to dinner, dancing, what?"

"Oh, no, Ms. Welham. This is a private celebration."

Her blood raced at the thought. "Invitation only?"

"Invitation only. Now get your butt out of this car and home. I've got a few errands to run, I need to pack so I can go directly to the airport from your place, and then I'll be there." He looked at his watch. "Give me three hours. I'll be there by five."

She saluted. "Yes, sir." She started to pull the door handle, but he grabbed her and pulled her back for one more breath-stealing kiss. "Five o'clock."

"Five o'clock."

His eyes smoked, his jaw tensed, his lips parted. "Don't dress up on my account."

"Okay."

"In fact, don't dress at all."

"Okay."

13

DARCY WAS TRYING very hard not to panic. After all, a takeover would probably be a very complicated affair. She knew Michael must be working hard to hammer out the details, so he most likely just didn't have the time to call her.

At least, that's what she kept telling herself.

He'd been gone for three days, and she hadn't heard a word. Many times she'd considered calling her father, just to say hi, just to check in, just to…check on Michael. Every time she'd put the phone down before she finished dialing. He wanted a future with her. He'd told her so. He'd contact her the first chance he got. She had to keep the faith.

But she didn't have to like it.

Their last night together had been a dream. Michael had spent the evening pampering her, loving her, worshipping her. She didn't know if it was normal for men and women to make love as many times as they had that night, but she knew she could get used to it.

In fact, since then her body felt lost and lonely without Michael's hands on it. She'd had three restless nights to miss him, to miss his scent, his touch, his voice.

Though the way he'd kissed her, looked at her, made love to her, had shouted promises of a future, he'd made no oral commitment to her. At the time she hadn't thought she'd needed verbal reassurances. Right now, she wished she had it in writing.

A shout from the kitchen brought her out of her misery. The noise continued, and she recognized it as the voice of their Italian chef. She couldn't understand the words, but the tone told her something was very, very wrong.

She left the break room to investigate.

Tom and the chef stood in the back kitchen, the chef shaking a finger at one of his assistants and talking nonstop in his native language.

"What's wrong?" Darcy asked Tom.

"From what I can gather, Luigi is upset," Tom said dryly.

"How observant of you."

"I think it has something to do with the private party tonight."

Darcy laid a hand on Luigi's arm and smiled down into his purple face. She considered advising him to picture her and Michael making love, but thought that might not work as well calming him as it did her. "What's wrong, Luigi?"

"Dis…dis *scemo* did not-a get-ta da shrimp for tonight's pasta. Where am I going ta get-ta fifty pounds of da fresha shrimp on such short notice, can you answer me dis?" He called Paul—the assistant—a few more choice Italian names. "Ruined. The night's menu is ruined!"

Tom and Paul both appeared a little pale. Luigi looked positively apoplectic. Darcy took a couple of breaths, and closed her eyes, picturing Michael as he looked when he was gazing down at her, a part of her. The mental image didn't exactly calm her, but it did boost her confidence.

"Maybe not," she said.

"But…but—"

She smiled. "Let's go see if we can revise the menu."

"The lady, she specifically requested my scampi!"

"Well, your scampi isn't going to taste all that terrific without shrimp in it. Let's go see what else we have."

Luigi sputtered some more, but he followed her to the walk-in refrigerator.

DARCY COLLAPSED into Tom's guest chair, exhausted but exhilarated. "Well, we survived!" she said, taking off her flats and rubbing her aching feet.

"Survived, hell, we triumphed!" Tom said, his face flushed with success. He patted Darcy on the shoulder. "Thanks to you, hon. That pasta dish was out of this world! Where'd you come up with that recipe?"

Darcy shrugged, although inside pride swelled. "I just looked at the ingredients we had and threw it together."

"Brilliant. Who'd have thought tuna, sun-dried tomatoes and pistachio nuts would taste that good together!"

"I'm glad Mrs. Fletcher finally came around. She was pretty upset there at first."

"How couldn't she? The pasta dish was everyone's favorite. Besides, I told a little white lie. I told her the shrimp just didn't meet our standards."

"Well, you're welcome to add the dish to your menu if you want."

Tom dropped into his chair. "Darcy, why would you give it up so easily?"

"What do you mean?"

"You've got a gift. Use it."

"How? Welham's will be a division of Dining Incorporated any day now."

Tom waved. "Right, June first. But I'm not talking about the restaurants—"

"June first?" Darcy interrupted. "How do you know that?"

"That's what the agreement says."

"The agreement? Are you saying—" Darcy swallowed "—the agreement's already been signed?"

"You didn't know?"

Shaking her head, she said, "When?"

"When was it signed?"

"Yes."

"Tuesday morning. It didn't take long, because they'd already worked out the terms. All that was really left to do was to cross the t's and dot the i's."

"It's done," Darcy whispered. Tuesday morning. And it was now Thursday night, and still no word from Michael.

"That's right, hon. And let me tell you, I think it was a

real smart decision on your part. I know your father's elated.''

''I...I'm glad.''

Tom stood and came around the desk. ''Well, I've got to get out there and make sure they're cleaning up the mess. That was some wild bunch for a fiftieth-wedding-anniversary party.''

Darcy smiled weakly. ''I...think I'll call my dad, if you don't mind. I'll be out in a minute.''

''Sure, hon, take your time.''

Heart pounding, Darcy called her apartment. When her machine picked up, she punched in the two-number code to retrieve her messages. The stupid machine told her no messages existed. She hung up.

Her hands were shaking now, so it took her four attempts to get her father's number right. He was usually in bed fairly early, but with the time difference it was still only seven o'clock in Spokane. He answered on the second ring.

''Hi, Daddy,'' she said, her voice cracking a little.

''Darcy?''

''Yeah, it's me.''

''Is something wrong, Princess?''

''I...just wanted to know how the takeover went.''

''Smooth as cream. Which reminds me. You and I need to get together with my accountant. You've got some big decisions you need to make about your finances, Princess.''

''Yeah, sure, Daddy,'' she answered absently. Her eyes lit on a clipboard with a yellow legal pad attached to it. With a pang she recognized Michael's handwriting. She pulled it to her.

''Is something wrong, sweetheart? You sound a little strange.''

Darcy smiled at the list on the top page. It was so like Michael to be organized like that. ''No, Daddy, I'm fine. I...just wanted to check in.''

''I'm glad.''

''I'm glad everything went well.''

''Me too, Princess. Palm Springs, here I come.''

Darcy forced a small laugh. Randomly she riffled through Michael's legal pad. "Well, I guess I need to go. I...love you, Daddy."

"Love you too, Princess. Come home soon."

"I will." She started to say goodbye, then stopped. "Daddy?"

"Hmm?"

"Is...Michael Davidson still in Spokane?"

"Nope, he hightailed it out of here before the ink was dry. I took him to the airport myself Tuesday morning. Nice young man."

"Yes. Yes, he is. Well, goodbye, Daddy."

Darcy hung up, staring into space. *Nice young man, is he? Then why the hell hasn't he called me?*

Darcy was torn. Should she just sit quietly and wait for Michael to come back for her? What other options did she have? She didn't have the courage to just call him and say...what? "I miss you. Why haven't you called me? Why the hell didn't you take the first flight back to D.C.?"

Maybe that was it. Maybe he was on his way to D.C. right now. It was possible. After all, he'd have to go to New York to deliver the contracts first. Maybe, even now, he was on a shuttle heading south.

The thought cheered her a little, but the uncertainty still gnawed at her belly. She had to know. She looked down at his pad again, her fingers tracing Michael's bold handwriting. Maybe there were notes in this pad that were important to him. Maybe he needed them, and couldn't remember where he'd left them.

She jumped up and moved around Tom's desk. Finding the phone book in the middle drawer, she flipped through it until she found the map with the area codes. Then she raced around the desk again and dialed directory assistance for the New York area.

When the lady answered, Darcy gave her Michael's name and street address, praying he wasn't unlisted.

He wasn't. As the electronic voice rattled off his number,

Darcy scrambled for a pen and wrote it down on Michael's pad.

She hung up slowly, taking a heaving breath. It was late, but Annie had already informed Darcy that she did most of her best work after midnight.

If Annie answered, she'd just tell her that Michael had left this pad in D.C., and she thought maybe there was important information on it he'd need.

With that in mind, she dialed the number. While she waited for a connection, she paged through the pad, hoping to find something, anything, that looked vitally important.

The phone rang once.

Darcy flipped pages. Lists of all sorts littered them, but none looked too urgent to her.

The phone rang a second time.

Darcy flipped another page. And stopped. Printed at the top were the words, *The Darcy Dilemma.*

"Davidson," an achingly familiar male voice barked.

Darcy stared at the page, stunned.

Flirting won't work.

Friendliness isn't working.

"Hello?"

Kissing her worked.

Get her alone.

Show her appreciation.

Kiss her.

Keep your damn tongue out of her mouth.

Her heart split into a million jagged pieces. She dropped into a chair, her legs no longer capable of supporting her.

"Is anyone there?"

Guilt works.

Jealousy works.

Darcy was almost surprised there wasn't a *Making love to her works real well* written there somewhere. Rage and an overwhelming hurt consumed her. Slowly, she replaced the receiver, physically and symbolically severing her connection to Michael Stephen Davidson.

MICHAEL HUNG UP the phone, a vague sense of unease teasing through him. He returned to the kitchen table and sat down across from Annie. "Crank call."

Annie nodded absently, then picked up the conversation where they'd left off when the phone rang. "If you get offered the job, you're going to take it?"

"I think so."

"It's less money."

"Yeah, but it costs a lot less to live in Spokane than it does here. Besides, the base pay may be less, but if I can turn profits around, the profit-sharing deal they outlined will more than make up for it."

Annie shook her head. "Why, Michael? I thought you were happy with D.I."

"I was. Or, I thought I was. But this last deal really opened my eyes, Annie. Darcy really opened my eyes. Somewhere along the line, I lost my scruples. You wouldn't believe what I was willing to do to win the deal."

He stood up and started pacing. "Then Darcy just handed it to me." He raked his fingers through his hair. "And I took it. I feel like the biggest bastard."

"You wanted it for the right reasons, big bro."

He spun back to face her. "Did I? Did I really?"

"Of course you did. You wanted it for Mom. For me."

He laughed harshly. "Yeah, what a great guy I am, huh? Sorry, Annie, that doesn't wash. I wanted this promotion for me. So I could come home and show everyone what a hotshot I was. I wanted it so I could send the write-up in *Business Week* to our grandfather. I wanted it to prove to him he was wrong about me."

Annie didn't have to ask what he was talking about. He'd told her about the confrontation with their grandfather several years earlier. "So what are you going to do now?"

"God, I don't know. I've felt so damn unclean the last couple of days, I haven't even been able to call her. If I get there and she's already regretting her decision, I don't know how I'll ever be able to look at myself in the mirror."

"This isn't just about tricking some heiress, is it? You really care about Darcy, don't you?"

Michael looked his little sister in the eye. "More than I thought it was possible to care." He grabbed his beer and took a healthy slug. "All I can do is promise to make her so happy, she'll never miss the restaurants. Problem is, I don't even know if I'm capable of that."

Annie put her hand on his arm. "From what I could tell, the woman is head over heels in love with you. My bet is, she'd take you over any old restaurant any old day."

"I hope you're right."

"I am. You should have seen the darling note she sent me after she finished my manuscript. She's got a romantic heart, Mike. Go for her."

He nodded. "I hear from Jake Hanley tomorrow morning. If I get offered the job, I'm taking the next flight to D.C."

"What if you don't get offered the job?"

Michael heaved a breath. "I don't know. I know Darcy hates New York. I don't think I could ask her to live here."

Annie grinned. "Wow, that sounds pretty permanent."

Michael glared at her. "Of course it's permanent. What do you think I've been talking about here?"

She pushed him back to the table, sat him down and handed him paper and a pencil. "Okay, bottom line is, you now hate this job."

"Yes."

"So if you don't get the other job, why not put yourself out on the market? Someone, somewhere, is bound to snap you up. Just make the stipulation that you don't want to stay in New York."

Michael started scribbling. For a daffy woman, Annie sure knew how to put things in perspective. He looked up. "If Mom and I move, you *are* coming with us, aren't you?"

Annie shrugged. "Have laptop, will travel."

Michael grinned for the first time in what felt like centuries. "I knew that laptop was a good investment."

"Now go invest in something for yourself. Like a dia-mond ring."

IF DARCY DIDN'T stop crying soon, she was going to flood her apartment. It made her mad that she was crying, any-way. She wasn't a crier, and she hated Michael for turning her into a blubbering idiot.

"Well, Darcy girl, what else did you expect?" she mut-tered, after blowing her nose. "You weren't actually foolish enough to believe a man like Michael could fall in love with you, were you?"

She snorted. "Of course you were. You never learn, do you?"

She looked down at the page she'd torn from Michael's pad last night. Why she'd kept it, she couldn't begin to fathom. Why she kept reading down the list, she didn't know either. It was torture. And yet, she had to keep re-minding herself that Michael Davidson was a low-life snake. Otherwise she'd do something really stupid. Like miss him. Like march on up to New York and demand that he love her. Like forgive him.

No, she'd never forgive him. Not in a million years. He'd used her. He'd seduced her, certain she'd fall right into his arms and into his bed. And then she'd stupidly hand him her restaurants on a silver platter. And what really galled Darcy was, she'd done *exactly* that. He'd made an utter fool of her. And the moment he'd gotten what he wanted, he'd disappeared.

The no-good, low-life, bug-eating frog.

Only, for a while there, her frog had turned into a prince. Or so she'd been fool enough to believe.

She tossed down the page and took a sip of iced tea. The doorbell rang. Listlessly, Darcy crossed the living room and looked through the peephole. Her iced tea fell from her suddenly boneless hand and crashed at her feet.

Heedless of the mess, she took a step back, lost her bal-ance and fell on her rump. She sat sprawled, unable to breathe, unable to control her racing heart.

What was he doing here? Why had he come? She couldn't face him now, not after discovering his dirty, low-down plan. Her dignity had been shattered enough. She couldn't stand the thought of him smirking at her, or worse, taking pity on her.

She sat perfectly still for she didn't know how long. He resorted to knocking. When she didn't respond, his voice drifted to her through the door.

"Darcy, I know you're in there. I heard the crash. Please open up."

She didn't even dare take a breath.

"Darcy, I'm sorry I haven't called. There were things I needed to take care of. But it's all done now." He paused. "I have some good news," he tossed out like bait to a fish.

"Go away!" she shouted.

There was another pause. "Why?"

"As if you didn't know!"

"Darcy, why is your voice coming from the floor? Did you fall?"

She scrambled to her feet, unfortunately cutting her hand on a shard of glass in the process. "Ouch!"

"What? What happened?"

Sucking on her palm, she said, "Just go away!"

"Not until you tell me what's wrong."

Darcy yanked open the door. "What's wrong, you double-crossing schmuck, is that I know all about your little scheme."

He cocked his head, but a strange look flew over his features. She'd almost call it dread. "What scheme?"

God, he was beautiful. Why did he have to be such a snake? Maybe Darcy had a personality flaw. Maybe she was really superficial. Because, knowing what she knew about him, she still wanted him. God, what a fool!

She stepped back. "Well, by all means, come on in and I'll show you what scheme."

He hesitated. "I really missed you, Darcy."

She snorted and spun on her heel. Marching to her coffee

table, she turned to glare at him over her shoulder. "Can it, Davidson. You can cut the act now."

She ran headlong into her brass apothecary lamp. It crashed to the floor, but Darcy ignored it, stepping over it on her mission.

She picked up the paper and turned, rustling it.

Michael bent over to pick up the lamp.

"Leave it!" she ordered. "I don't want your help, Michael. With anything."

He straightened slowly. "What in hell is going on?"

Thrusting the paper at him, she snarled, "This, you slithering—"

"I get the idea," he said, cutting her off. He took the paper from her, then glared down at it. His glare disappeared in a flash, and dismay took its place. He whispered an obscenity.

Looking up, his blue eyes appeared genuinely contrite. Well, add acting to his many talents.

"I can explain."

"The list seems pretty self-explanatory, so don't waste your breath. Or my time."

"Darcy, please—"

Something burst inside of her. All of her hurt, her raw, aching emotion came tumbling out. "No! Don't make things worse!" She snatched the list from him and shredded it. "You used me!"

"No, I—"

"I was a means to an end for you. You wanted that acquisition, and you'd stop at nothing to get it. Lucky for you the only obstacle in your path was poor, pathetic, gullible Darcy."

"That's not—"

"God, how you must have laughed all the way to Spokane."

He took her shoulders. "Listen to me. That's not true!"

Darcy shrugged off his hands. "Don't touch me! You're just like Brad Fontaine."

Almost laughably, he looked insulted by that remark. He

opened his mouth, but she beat him to the punch again. "Was that little scenario up in New York planned, Michael? How brilliant. How sneaky. How low, to bring your family in on your little schemes."

Blood drained from his face. "My family had nothing to do with it."

"No, I'm sure they didn't. They seemed too nice for that. You're the snake in that crowd. You probably just hinted what you wanted them to say to me."

"No!" he shouted. The guilt had left his face, and now he only looked angry.

Well, that was good. She was angry too. That self-righteous anger and humiliation were the only things keeping her from throwing herself into his arms and pleading with him to tell her it was a joke. That they were on *Candid Camera* and their prize was a honeymoon trip to the Bahamas.

"Get out, Michael," she said, her voice low. She was seriously close to having a nervous breakdown, and she didn't want him to witness it.

"Dammit, Darcy! Yes, it may have started out that way. But what we had turned into something much more."

"*Had* seems to be the operative word here."

He jerked her into his arms. Right where she did and didn't want to be. "We could still have it," he said, his eyes smoky and pleading. "Please, Darcy."

His lips lowered dangerously. Darcy shoved him away. "Guess what, Michael. This time kissing her isn't going to work."

The fight seemed to drain from him. His shoulders, if possible, deflated. "I'm sorry, Darcy. I never meant to hurt you."

Hysterical laughter threatened to burst forth from her. "No, I'm sure you didn't. It wasn't on the list. You also didn't mean to humiliate me. Make a fool out of me. Not...on...the...list." She threw the shredded paper against his chest. "You just meant to use me."

He flinched as if she'd slapped him. After taking several

deep breaths, he gazed at her so sadly that she almost started crying. Then he turned, silently, and walked to the door, crunching through the glass without caring.

He started out, then turned back to her. "Falling in love with you wasn't on the list, either. Unfortunately for me, that happened too. Goodbye, Darcy."

14

SPOKANE WAS Darcy's hometown. She should have found comfort returning to it, wrapping the arid, mountainous beauty around her and letting it soothe her. She should have marveled at the majestic ponderosa pines, enjoyed the perfumy scent of the lilac bushes that were in full bloom in mid-May.

She should have laughed at the squirrels in Cour D'Alene Park, who had welcomed her back happily at the first sign of peanuts. She should have settled into her Browne's Addition apartment—actually the entire third floor of a refurbished old mansion—easily, content to be near her father again. Content to be back where she belonged.

All she felt was a bottomless emptiness.

She'd been home just over a month. In that time, a dizzying number of things had happened to her. Thanks to Tom Murphy, she was now an independent Menu Consultant for Dining Incorporated.

Tom had given the word to the higher-ups at D.I. that Darcy possessed some kind of gift with food. After he'd served them her pasta recipe as proof, he'd convinced them that Darcy could work wonders at a variety of their restaurant chains. They'd contacted her the day after her phone had been connected, and after consulting with her father, Darcy had given them her terms. Amazingly, they'd eagerly agreed.

So now she had a career. One she loved, so she had no complaints there. Still, she found it infinitely ironic that she now charged an outrageous fee to the company who had given her, then taken away, Michael Davidson.

If he knew about her new relationship with D.I. he wasn't saying. She hadn't heard from him since the day—almost two months ago—he'd walked out of her apartment and out of her life.

She'd almost gone after him that day. But she hadn't. For a week she'd agonized over whether she'd made a horrible mistake by not fighting for him. But when two weeks had passed and he hadn't tried to see her again, she'd come to the conclusion that what she'd actually done was given Michael his out. That's when she made plans to move home.

His declaration of love had been alms to the poor. He'd had enough of a conscience to feel guilty, and he'd wanted to offer that crumb. But he obviously hadn't wanted to fight for their relationship.

Relationship? What relationship? They had sex a few times. That didn't constitute a relationship. In fact, she had to give Michael credit for at least that much honesty. He'd told her up front that if she was looking for long-term, she should look somewhere else.

But the scum didn't have to profess a love he didn't feel. She hadn't asked him to. Now she wished she'd laughed in his face. But she hadn't. She'd just stared at him as he'd turned and walked away. Then had held out false, stupid hopes that he'd come back and try to change her mind.

Darcy shook her head as the squirrel she'd named Foxy put his front paws on her knee and chattered noisily.

She smiled weakly. "Okay, big boy, the last one's for you." She gave him the peanut and laughed softly as he tore the shell apart to get to the meaty nut. He instantly came back for more, but she held out her hands. "That's it for today."

Foxy chattered his disgust, then hopped away.

"Typical fickle man," she whispered, her throat closing.

She stood up, brushing debris from the seat of her shorts. Strolling to the trash can to toss the empty bag, she looked out over the sun-dappled loveliness of the park and sighed.

She had work to do. Her current project was revamping

the menu for a chain of Italian restaurants owned by D.I. Amazingly enough, she'd actually learned to cook. She could now test the recipes first. Her office was her state-of-the-art kitchen, and nothing soothed her melancholy more than getting lost in the logistics of making a dish, then experimenting with the ingredients to make it delicious when cooked in large quantities.

At least she had that, she thought, as she crossed Cour D'Alene Street. She looked to the left. And stopped dead in the middle of the street. A man half a block away reminded her so much of Michael, it took her breath away. He was the right height, with the same slightly unruly, pitch-black hair. The shoulders were the same sexy breadth, and the man even had the nerve to be wearing a tailored suit. He had sunglasses on, so she couldn't see his eyes, but somehow she knew the man's eyes would be blue.

A honking horn made her jump, and she hurried the rest of the way across the street. At the sidewalk she looked back. The man was gone.

Why that left her bereft was a mystery. Obviously, the man hadn't been Michael. He was a full continent away, happily getting on with his yuppie life. For all she knew, the man she'd seen was a mirage, or in actuality had blond hair and was a midget. She'd just projected Michael's image onto him.

As she reached the front entrance to her home, Darcy clucked in self-disgust. She had to stop dwelling on Michael. She just had to. If she didn't, she'd end up a patient in Eastern State Hospital.

An hour later, Darcy shoved an experimental recipe for baked caper and cheese ravioli into the oven and set the timer for an hour. She washed the flour from her hands, grabbed a soda from the refrigerator, then sat down at her small wood block table to read the *Spokesman-Review*.

She read through the national and international news, then started to flip through the business section. She turned the page, then froze. Slowly, several heartbeats later, she flipped it back.

Smiling at her from the front page of the business section was Michael Davidson. She was so mired in shock, it took her a full minute to register the headline beside his photograph.

"Davidson Named President of Everything Kitchen."

Everything Kitchen was the name of the largest chain of kitchen-gadget stores in the country. It was also a multimillion dollar *Spokane-based* corporation. And according to the article, Michael Davidson, *her* Michael Davidson, had taken over the reins of the faltering company.

The article went on to say that Davidson would be holding a press conference the next day at noon in the lobby of Everything Kitchen's Riverside building. He planned to outline his restructuring strategy for the company, and to also reassure stockholders and employees alike that their investments and jobs were secure.

Darcy couldn't breathe. She couldn't think. She couldn't move. Shock held her immobile, imbecilic and breathless.

Michael had moved to Spokane. He'd left New York and moved to Spokane. He'd left Dining Incorporated and moved to Spokane.

Coincidence? Yes, it had to be. She couldn't allow it to mean more than that. She wouldn't. She couldn't live through another heartbreaking experience. She'd never, ever survive it.

But the knowledge that they shared the same town, the same streets, the same air made her dizzy and nauseous. How could she live here, knowing that at any moment of any day, she might run into him?

How would he react? she wondered. Would he engage in polite, yet distant, chitchat? Or would he be so uncomfortable that he'd just look right through her and pretend not to know her?

Did he know she'd moved back here? Or did he think she'd settled permanently in D.C.?

So many questions rattled through her head. She didn't know how long she sat and stared at his picture. About an hour, she decided, when the timer started dinging at her.

In a trance, she went to the oven and removed the crispy-baked ravioli. She put three samples on her plate, one covered with a white sauce, one with a marinara sauce, one with a spinach sauce, then took it back to the table.

While she stared at Michael, she took a bite of each in turn, washing her palette clean with lemon water between tastes. When she'd tried all three, she realized she hadn't tasted any of them. Her taste buds were as much in shock as the rest of her.

Shaken, she dumped the plate into the sink, turned and hugged herself. It was too much. How dare the man invade her territory? How dare he move to her hometown? How dare he be so damn photogenic?

She might have continued listing her grievances against him, if a knock at her door hadn't brought her up short. Her heart leapt to her throat. Who could it be? Darcy almost never had visitors. She was as much a loner now as she'd been most of her life. Except for those few weeks...

She tried to calm her raging nerves as she went to the door. It wasn't Michael, she was sure. Maybe it was some Jehovah's Witnesses. Or the Mormons. Maybe it was some Girl Scouts, selling cookies. Was this Girl Scout cookie season? Whatever, it wouldn't be Michael.

She was right. It wasn't Michael. It wasn't a Jehovah's Witness or a Girl Scout either, but the disappointment that washed through her because it wasn't Michael was a real blow. She didn't have time to think about it, though, considering a kid she recognized from the neighborhood stood at her door with a golden retriever puppy in his arms.

Darcy plastered a smile on her face. "What an adorable puppy!" she said, scruffing the dog's head. "What can I do for you?"

The kid thrust the dog at Darcy, startling her. "She's for you."

"Excuse me?"

"The puppy's for you."

"I...don't understand. I didn't buy a puppy."

''Nah, it's a gift. Some old guy paid me a buck to deliver her. She's a girl.''

Confused, Darcy took the puppy. ''Some old guy?''

''Yeah. There's a card under her collar. Here, see?'' the boy said, pointing to a small card. ''Some of the bigger guys are coming any time now to bring stuff for her.''

The puppy wiggled and licked Darcy's chin. She instantly fell in love with the little white-blond fur ball. Still she didn't understand. But before she could question the boy further, he said, ''Have fun!'' and scampered down the hall.

Dazed, Darcy watched as three more boys appeared, carting a metal crate, a huge bag of puppy food, toys and rawhides, a food bowl, a leash, a brush and a pooper-scooper. When they finished carrying it all in and dumping the treasures in her foyer, they left, whooping the whole way down the hall.

Darcy closed the door, then carried the dog to the couch and sat down. The puppy immediately tried to climb up her chest to lick her face, its tail wagging furiously.

Darcy laughed, pulling the card from under the bright red collar. While trying to entertain the puppy, she took the note from the envelope and read it.

''It's about time you got a dog.''

It wasn't signed, and she didn't recognize the handwriting. She immediately thought of Michael, but discarded the notion. Surely he wouldn't get her a dog.

Or would he? Was this just one more handout to assuage his guilty conscience?

But the little boy's words came back to her. An ''old guy'' had asked him to deliver it. Her father?

She didn't know, and at the moment she didn't care. She was too busy falling head over heels in love with the most adorable puppy she'd ever seen.

Darcy put the puppy on the floor and played with her for she didn't know how long. Then she took the pup across the street to the park, pooper-scooper and leash in her free hand. Setting the curious puppy on the grass, she snapped the leash on the collar and let her roam at will.

First things first. Darcy needed a name for her. She discarded Buttercup and Princess. Too sissy for her puppy. The puppy yipped, a high-pitched bark that came out sounding suspiciously like "Ralph."

Dropping to the ground and sitting Indian style, she let the puppy climb all over her. "How does Ralph sound?"

"Ralph!" the puppy agreed.

"It's not very feminine, certainly not traditional, but since neither of us are much of those things, I guess we might get away with it. What do you think?"

"Ralph!"

"Ralph it is."

She hugged the puppy, so thrilled at the gift from her unknown benefactor, she thought her heart would burst. Why hadn't she thought of this herself? A puppy on which to lavish all the love pent up inside her. It was perfect.

She and Ralph roamed the park a little while longer, and Darcy blessed her gift-giver when the pooper-scooper came in handy. Whoever it was, he'd certainly covered the bases.

They returned to the apartment a half hour later, when Ralph showed definite signs of slowing down. Darcy set up the crate in the kitchen and placed blankets on the metal bottom. To her amazement, the puppy almost looked grateful as she climbed in, turned in a circle twice, then plopped down and fell instantly to sleep.

Half relieved, half disappointed, Darcy left the kitchen. She picked up the cordless phone on the bookshelf and dialed her father's number.

When he answered, she got right to the point. "Daddy, did you buy me a dog?"

"What?"

"A dog. Did you have one delivered to me this afternoon?"

"No," he said slowly. "Are you saying someone gave you a dog?"

"A puppy," she said, almost elated. The dog had to have

come from Michael. Surprisingly, the thought didn't bother her. Somehow she knew he wasn't just trying to buy her forgiveness. Somehow she knew he was trying to tell her he still had faith in her, even if she'd lost faith in herself.

"She's a golden retriever," Darcy added breathlessly. "Her papers say she's ten weeks old and she's had her first shots. I named her Ralph."

"Whoa, slow down, sweetheart. Who would buy you a dog without asking you?"

"Someone who knew how much I've always wanted one."

There was a pause. "By the happy sound of your voice, I wish it *had* been me. Who do you suppose it was?"

"An old friend," Darcy answered, hoping he wouldn't probe.

Thankfully, he left it at that. "Ralph? You named a sweet female puppy Ralph?"

"Yes. Isn't it perfect?"

Her dad chuckled. "I guess it is, at that. Well, Princess, enjoy her. And good luck on the housebreaking. I'd love to come see her soon, but right now I've got to make my tee-off time at Indian Hills."

"Daddy, wait!"

"Hmm?"

"Did you...did you see in the paper that Michael Davidson was named president of Everything Kitchen?"

"I did indeed. As a matter of fact, I recommended him for the job."

Her heart sank. "You?"

"That's right. To tell you the truth, I really liked the young man right from the start. He's smart and savvy. But it was more. He was extremely concerned about how you really felt about the takeover. He showed heart. Since I knew his promotion hinged on the deal, I found it admirable that he wasn't thinking of himself first. And since I knew Ted was looking for a new..."

Her father's voice faded beneath the drone in Darcy's head. Michael had been worried about her feelings. He'd seemed more concerned about her than him and his promotion.

Oh, Michael!

Of course, that didn't mean he loved her. But it did show that he'd cared.

"...get out of New York."

"What?" she said, trying to hone in on her father's voice.

"I said, he expressed a real interest in getting out of New York. Told me his lady friend hated New York, and he hated asking her to live there. And when I approached him about a move to Spokane, he was delighted. Said he had a feeling his lady would like that a lot." There was a pause. "Hey, wait a minute. His lady friend wouldn't happen to be—"

"Daddy, I need to go."

"Darcy—"

"I'll explain everything later. Right now I need to think."

"Just tell me this. Are you his lady friend?"

"I was. But I think I blew it," she added glumly.

Amazingly, her father yelled "Ye-haw!" right into the phone. "Go get him, Darcy. If you could have seen the way his eyes lit up when he talked about you. Go get him."

"What if he's changed his mind?"

"Do you think he's the one who sent you the dog?"

"If it wasn't you, it had to be. He's the only one who...I told my goldfish story to."

"Go get him. At least try, Darce. You'll never know if you don't try."

Her heart was racing. Her father was right. If she didn't try, she'd never know. For once in her life, Darcy had to take a leap, and hope she landed on her feet. Or better yet, in Michael's arms. "I'll try."

"Way to go, Princess!"

"I'm scared, Daddy."

"I don't blame you. But I think your fears are unfounded in this case." There was a short, profound silence. Then he added, almost in a whisper. "And Darcy? I heartily approve."

Darcy hung up, her nerves strung to their snapping point. Hands shaking, she replaced the receiver and went to the kitchen to check on Ralph. The puppy was still sleeping, her eyes and paws twitching as she chased down some squirrel in her dreams.

Darcy's gaze fell to the newspaper, and Michael's picture. She moved to it, tracing the contours of his smiling lips. She read the article again. Then she got a pencil and paper and started to plan.

She drew up a list.

MICHAEL STOOD at the podium, making his speech. It was a good thing he'd memorized it, because his mind was so far from profit margins and organizational restructuring, he didn't even know what he was saying.

Yesterday, as he'd stood under one of the majestic oaks and watched Darcy feed squirrels, his heart had ached with all he'd lost. Him and his damn lists. When it came to his personal life, he was never going to make a list again, as long as he lived. He was going to learn to live for the moment, take what happiness he could find without analyzing it, fall in love like normal men did.

Just as soon as he got over Darcy.

Which, at current calculations, would happen sometime in the second quarter of the twenty-first century.

Yesterday, he'd mentally thrown all his lists away. No well-planned course of action was going to get Darcy back. So the only thing left to him was to follow his heart. And his heart had told him he wanted to do something to wipe the haunted, melancholy look from Darcy's features.

With that in mind, he'd scoured the pets section of the paper. Luck had been with him when he'd found golden puppies right near his new home on the South Hill.

After he'd paid the boys to deliver the puppy and supplies, he'd stuck around, knowing Darcy would come out eventually to walk the puppy. The ache in his heart had eased somewhat when he'd seen her joyful expression as she followed the wandering puppy around the park. When she'd sat down in the grass and allowed the puppy to climb all over her, Michael had actually laughed for the first time in two months.

He'd felt fairly certain that she'd figure out who sent her the puppy, but he knew it wouldn't change anything. That had been confirmed somewhat when he'd received a philodendron this morning with a card that said, "Thank you for Ralph. I love her." That note hadn't been signed. But the next one that came with the rubber plant and said, "Congratulations. Everything Kitchen is lucky to have you," had been. It said simply, "Darcy." No "Love, Darcy," but what did he expect?

Exactly one hour later—an hour ago—he'd received one final plant. This one a hanging spider. This card said, "Welcome to Spokane. Darcy."

Along with the plants he'd already brought to his new office, he now felt he was working in a greenhouse. And he loved it.

Trying to bring his focus back to the speech at hand, he glanced down at the notes he really didn't need. When he looked up, a photographer snapped a picture, its flash momentarily blinding him. But he kept right on talking as he blinked away the large spots before his eyes. He just wanted to get this over with and get off the stage.

As his vision cleared, he gazed out over the lobby at the twenty or so business reporters from the various news media. A fairly large turnout. But he supposed that the health of his company was of major concern to the locals, as well as the national business scene. He took a breath and went on talking.

"Downsizing is not necessarily an answer in our case. We're already a lean, well-oiled machine, and we value all of our personnel highly. What we're looking to do is re-evaluate some store loca—"

Darcy.

She stood near the glass doors to the building, looking

fresh as a spring flower in a flowing peasant dress. Her hair was loose, the way he liked it, her shoulders and legs bare. She had open-toed sandals on her feet, and even from here he could see that her toenails were painted coral.

She held her puppy in one arm. When she realized she'd caught his attention, she smiled.

Michael was struck dumb, his speech forgotten. That wasn't a friendly smile. That wasn't a polite smile. That was a smile that whispered, "I love you."

The rest of the world sank in on itself. Nothing existed but Darcy.

She lifted one of the puppy's front paws and waved it at Michael, bringing him out of his stunned elation.

"Excuse me," he croaked, then came out from behind the podium, ignoring the murmurs from the reporters.

He traveled in a direct path to Darcy, never taking his eyes from hers. Her eyes widened for a moment, before narrowing over a devastating grin.

When he reached her, he didn't say a word. He just took her in his arms and kissed her. Her response was instantaneous and cataclysmic. His world caught fire, burning bright and beautiful.

The softness, the taste of the lips he couldn't forget, the scent of the woman who'd haunted his dreams, the silk of the skin he'd had such a short time to worship, all hit him with the force of a speeding truck.

Darcy, his Darcy, was back. And this time he'd never let her go.

He suddenly became aware of something wet and rough under his chin. That brought him to a semblance of his senses. Which was why he finally registered that the small crowd had broken out in loud applause, several wolf whistles, and a few shocked gasps.

Reluctantly he broke the kiss and looked down at her. God, to have her this close after such a long, long time without her was overwhelming.

He said the first thing that came into his mind. "It sure

would be nice if Ralph is housebroken by the time we get married.''

IN POINT OF FACT, Ralph hadn't been housebroken by the time they were married, two weeks later. In point of fact, it took nearly two months to housebreak her completely. But as Darcy pointed out, it would take their children much longer.

And it had.

Krissie, their oldest, took two years to train. Kyle had been a stubborn little cuss. It took nearly three years to convince him that the toilet wouldn't eat him. But Katie, their youngest, was out of diapers by eighteen months.

As he stood in the doorway to the kitchen, watching Darcy juggle the children and step over the dog, all the while arguing with a chef on the phone, Michael smiled, his heart bursting with the raw, powerful emotion that was his love for his wife and family. Once again he threw up a silent prayer of thanks to the patron saint of matrimony—if there was such a thing. He was blessed. He knew it, and he thanked God for it.

Falling for Darcy had been the smartest thing he'd ever done. And damn if he hadn't fallen hard.

And often.

LOVE & LAUGH

INTO AUGUST!

#25 LADY ON TOP
Judy Griffith Gill

Librarian Ali Kozinski thinks she should have been named "Polly Predictable." Heck, her neighbors even know her gardening schedule! So when a sexy photojournalist moves in next door, her first step in her new assertiveness training is to seduce him. And then to seduce him again. Keith Devon isn't sure what hit him, but the girl next door sure is friendly. He's beginning to think he's found the sweet girl of his dreams when he learns that he's just part of her program....

#26 RIGHT CHEST, WRONG NAME
Colleen Collins

Professor Russell Harrington wakes up after his bachelor party with a terrible hangover, little memory of the evening before and a tattoo with the name Liz on his chest. *Liz* isn't the name of his very proper fiancée. Even worse, Russell can't seem to keep a shirt on his chest as he searches for the mystery woman. He fears that not only has Liz branded him, but that she's also stolen his heart. So who is she?

Chuckles available now:

#23 WHO'S BEEN SLEEPING IN MY BED?
Jule McBride
#24 THE HARDER THEY FALL
Trish Jensen

Take 4 bestselling love stories FREE

Plus get a FREE surprise gift!

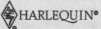

As Seen on TV!

Free Gift Offer

With a Free Gift proof-of-purchase
from any Harlequin® book, you can receive
a beautiful cubic zirconia pendant.

This stunning marquise-shaped stone is a genuine cubic
zirconia—accented by an 18" gold tone necklace.
(Approximate retail value $19.95)

Send for yours today...
compliments of ✦ HARLEQUIN®

To receive your free gift, a cubic zirconia pendant, send us one original proof-of-purchase, photocopies not accepted, from the back of any Harlequin Romance®, Harlequin Presents®, Harlequin Temptation®, Harlequin Superromance®, Harlequin Intrigue®, Harlequin American Romance®, or Harlequin Historicals® title available at your favorite retail outlet, together with the Free Gift Certificate, plus a check or money order for $1.65 U.S./$2.15 CAN. (do not send cash) to cover postage and handling, payable to Harlequin Free Gift Offer. We will send you the specified gift. Allow 6 to 8 weeks for delivery. Offer good until December 31, 1997, or while quantities last. Offer valid in the U.S. and Canada only.

Free Gift Certificate

Name: _____

Address: _____

City: _____ State/Province: _____ Zip/Postal Code: _____

Mail this certificate, one proof-of-purchase and a check or money order for postage and handling to: HARLEQUIN FREE GIFT OFFER 1997. In the U.S.: 3010 Walden Avenue, P.O. Box 9071, Buffalo NY 14269-9057. In Canada: P.O. Box 604, Fort Erie, Ontario L2Z 5X3.

FREE GIFT OFFER   084-KEZ

ONE PROOF-OF-PURCHASE
To collect your fabulous FREE GIFT, a cubic zirconia pendant, you must include this original proof-of-purchase for each gift with the properly completed Free Gift Certificate.

084-KEZR

LOVE & LAUGHTER LET'S CELEBRATE SWEEPSTAKES
OFFICIAL RULES—NO PURCHASE NECESSARY

To enter, complete an Official Entry Form or 3" x 5" card by hand printing the words "Love & Laughter Let's Celebrate Sweepstakes," your name and address thereon and mailing it to: in the U.S., Love & Laughter Let's Celebrate Sweepstakes, P.O. Box 9076, Buffalo, NY 14269-9076, or in Canada to, Love & Laughter Let's Celebrate Sweepstakes, P.O. Box 637, Fort Erie, Ontario L2A 5X3. Limit: one entry per envelope, one prize to an individual, family or organization. Entries must be sent via first-class mail and be received no later than 11/30/97. No liability is assumed for lost, late, misdirected or nondelivered mail.

Three (3) winners will be selected in a random drawing (to be conducted no later than 12/31/97) from among all eligible entries received by D. L. Blair, Inc., an independent judging organization whose decisions are final, to each receive a collection of 15 Love & Laughter Romantic Comedy videos (approximate retail value: $250 U.S. per collection).

Sweepstakes offer is open only to residents of the U.S. (except Puerto Rico) and Canada who are 18 years of age or older, except employees and immediate family members of Harelquin Enterprises, Ltd., their affiliates, subsidiaries, and all other agencies, entities and persons connected with the use, marketing or conduct of this sweepstakes. All applicable laws and regulations apply. Offer void wherever prohibited by law. Taxes and/or duties on prizes are the sole responsibility of the winners. Any litigation within the province of Quebec respecting the conduct and awarding of prize may be submitted to the Régie des alcools, des courses et des jeux. All prizes will be awarded; winners will be notified by mail. No substitution for prizes is permitted. Odds of winning are dependent upon the number of eligible entries received.

Any prize or prize notification returned as undeliverable may result in the awarding of that prize to an alternative winner. By acceptance of their prize, winners consent to use of their names, photographs or likenesses for purposes of advertising, trade and promotion on behalf of Harelquin Enterprises, Ltd., without further compensation unless prohibited by law. In order to win a prize, residents of Canada will be required to correctly answer a time-limited, arithmetical skill-testing question administered by mail.

For a list of winners (available after December 31, 1997), send a separate stamped, self-addressed envelope to: Love & Laughter Let's Celebrate Sweepstakes Winner, P.O. Box 4200, Blair, NE 68009-4200, U.S.A.

LLRULES

Celebrate with
LOVE & LAUGHTER™

Love to watch movies?

Enter now to win a FREE 15-copy video collection of romantic comedies in Love & Laughter's Let's Celebrate Sweepstakes.

WIN A ROMANTIC COMEDY VIDEO COLLECTION!

To enter the Love & Laughter Let's Celebrate Sweepstakes, complete an Official Entry Form or hand print on a 3" x 5" card the words "Love & Laughter Let's Celebrate Sweepstakes," your name and address and mail to: "Love & Laughter Let's Celebrate Sweepstakes," in the U.S., 3010 Walden Avenue, P.O. Box 9076, Buffalo, N.Y. 14269-9076; in Canada, P.O. Box 637, Fort Erie, Ontario L2A 5X3. Limit: one entry per envelope, one prize to an individual family or organization. Entries must be sent via first-class mail and be received no later than November 30, 1997. See back page ad for complete sweepstakes rules.

Celebrate with Love & Laughter™!

Official Entry Form

"Please enter me in the Love & Laughter Let's Celebrate Sweepstakes"

Name: _____

Address: _____

City: _____

State/Prov.: _____ Zip/Postal Code: _____

LLENTRY
